## KATHERINE

Cool. Serene. Beautiful. A child of wealth and status. All her life her mind had concealed certain longings from her body—until the night the fury broke free.

## SANDRA

Cunning. Sensual. Self-indulgent. All that Katherine was, she was not. But she was ready to take control—as soon as Katherine surrendered it.

Then a sudden cataclysmic act loosed an irresistible urge—an urge that would need to be satisfied again. . . .

## THRILL

The jolting novel of a blood passion.

# THRILL

by Barbara Petty

A DELL BOOK

Published by
Dell Publishing Co., Inc.
1 Dag Hammarskjold Plaza
New York, New York 10017

Dell ® TM 681510, Dell Publishing Co., Inc.

ISBN: 0-440-15295-X

Printed in the United States of America

First printing—April 1977

*For my parents,
my brother,
and, especially,
Steve*

# PROLOGUE

Sunday night and bone-chilling cold, a nasty November evening in New York. It was nearly eight o'clock when Barry Goldman trudged up the steps to his second-floor apartment. He shifted his weekend bag to his free hand and flipped through his keys until he found the right one. Inserting it into the lock, he twisted it to the left and instantly knew something was wrong. The door had opened too easily, it had not been double-locked. This was the first time in all the months he had lived with Ted that his roommate had left the door like that.

*Oh, Christ, we've been robbed,* he thought as he pushed the door open, expecting to see the apartment stripped bare of all its valuables. But the living room was undisturbed, nothing was missing. And Ted must be home because the lights and the stereo receiver were on.

Goldman breathed a sigh of relief as he stepped inside. But the next air he drew into his lungs sent icy fear traveling down his spine. There was a pungent smell pervading the apartment. It was only faint, but there was something loathsome about it that turned his stomach. It smelled of decay.

Trying to shake off his sense of foreboding, Goldman set down his bag. *It's only garbage,* he told himself. Or maybe some spoiled meat that Ted hadn't gotten around to throwing out.

He strode into the kitchen, determined to find the source of the offending odor and get rid of it. But there was nothing, and as he sniffed the air he realized that the smell was not coming from this part of the apartment.

He walked back into the living room and looked around, puzzled. From where he was standing he could see that Ted's door was ajar. "Hey, Ted," he called out, trying to make a joke of the situation, "what the hell you been smoking? It smells like shit."

He waited, expecting to hear Ted's voice come back with some wise-ass remark. There was no answer.

It was then that Goldman became aware of how unnaturally still the apartment seemed. It frightened him even more than the smell.

Feigning a bravado he did not feel, he sauntered over to his roommate's door and knocked on it sharply with his knuckles. "Ted! You there?" The eerie silence came back at him, mocking the false heartiness in his voice.

With the tips of his fingers he pushed the door farther ajar. Just as he started to call out his roommate's name again he saw the thing on the bed, and the sound died in his throat.

What had once been a human being was now a mass of white, waxy flesh sprawled face down across the foot of the bed, with a large rust-colored stain on its back and purplish legs dangling over the edge.

Gripping the doorknob with both trembling hands, Goldman pulled it shut with a violent heave. The odor was so dense now that it was almost palpable, and he could feel it stinging against his nostrils—foul, putrid, the smell of death.

Gagging and choking and trying not to retch, he stumbled into his bedroom and reached for the phone. Clutching at the receiver, he dialed 911, the police emergency number.

The voice on the other end seemed indifferent and casual, and filled him with a terrible, frustrating sense of isolation. "Don't you understand?" he shouted into the phone. "It's a *murder!* My roommate is dead!"

He was surprised by his own words. Until that moment he had not admitted to himself that the corpse must be Ted. Now he was sure it was. Who else could it be?

He hung up the phone, made a lunge for his bathroom, and vomited until there was nothing left in his stomach.

# CHAPTER ONE

Katherine Fielding ran her fingers nervously through her short hair and flicked a tiny speck of lint off the front of her sweater as she paused outside the door of her publisher's office.

This was the moment of truth. Now the weeks of waiting were over, and she'd soon find out whether or not she'd get her promotion. *Damn that Charles*, she thought. It was just like him, putting her off until the last possible minute on Friday afternoon. *Okay, let's get this over with,* she said to herself, gritting her teeth as she walked into his outer office.

Ellie, Charles's secretary, looked up indifferently. "Go on in," she said. "He's waiting for you."

Charles smiled broadly at Katherine as she walked through the door. "Here she is," he said. "The most beautiful girl on my staff."

"Hello, Charles," Katherine said coolly, sitting down across the desk from him.

Charles leaned back in his chair and folded his hands behind his head. "I never can appeal to your vanity, can I?" he said wryly. "Right now I bet you're saying to yourself, 'I wish he'd cut the crap and get down to business.'"

Katherine gazed levelly back at him. For once, he was right.

"Okay," he said, pushing himself forward. "I'll give it to you straight, Katherine. You didn't get the job."

Katherine blinked. She had known it was coming, but she still couldn't believe it. That little runt, that paunchy, balding, middle-aged playboy had screwed her again.

"Why not?" she asked, straining to keep her voice calm.

"Well, it's not for the reason you're thinking," Charles said defensively. "It's not because you're a woman."

*Like hell it isn't,* Katherine thought bitterly. But she said nothing.

Charles picked up a pencil and tapped it against the top of his desk. "I just don't think you're ready for that job yet, Katherine. That's what it comes down to."

Katherine lowered her eyes and stared down at her hands. She didn't want him to see how deeply he had cut her.

"Look, you're young yet," he said. "Hell, what are you? Thirty? You've got a great future in front of you, why rush it? There's still plenty of time for you to get to be associate editor."

Katherine groaned inwardly. He had given her this same line of bullshit when he'd turned her down the last time, when she had first tried for her present position, assistant editor on *Trend* magazine. Of course, later on—and long overdue —he had given her the promotion.

But this time it was not to be. Maybe never.

And she believed that this man, Charles Roth, this pompous son of a bitch, was the reason. Perhaps Katherine *was* especially ambitious, but she really believed that Charles was inferior. She had graduated magna cum laude from Smith and she had a master's degree from the Columbia School of Journalism, but the knowledge didn't make her feel any better. Worthless paper as far as Charles was concerned. It would no doubt please him to think that he had power over a woman who was so obviously smarter than he was. She had used her brains to get where she was; he had merely inherited his position.

Charles seemed ready to end the interview. He pushed back his chair and started to come around the desk. But then a strange, twisted smile came over his face.

"By the way," he said, "you might be interested in knowing who did get the job. It was Bruce— Bruce Youngman."

At her gasp of outrage, he seemed a little embarrassed. "Well, uh, I realize that you probably don't think he's better qualified than you are," Charles hedged, "but believe me, Katherine, I know what I'm doing." Then he smiled that smug, patronizing smile again.

Katherine was stunned. She couldn't look at him. She sat back in her chair and stared out at the darkening skyline of the city behind him. And then she became enraged. Bruce was a second-rate editor—and she was sure that Charles knew it, too.

He shifted his feet. She didn't care that she was making him uncomfortable—she would have

sat there all night if she thought it would really
bother him. But telling herself she was being
childish, she stood up and, averting her eyes,
walked toward the door.

"Hey, Katherine, don't take it so hard." He was
attempting to sound sincere, but it only made his
words seem more mocking. "Your turn will come
—if you stick with it." Katherine wondered if he
was trying to tell her to give it up. She thought
she would kill him.

Instead, she gave Ellie her best smile and went
on out into the corridor. She started back toward
her own office, then came to a sudden stop. The
only person she wanted to see just now was
Sandra. She couldn't face anyone in her own department, not yet, and she needed to talk to
someone—to vent her rage a little. She did an
abrupt about-face and headed for the library.

All the executives had their offices on this corridor, and as Katherine passed them she could
see that most of the offices were already dark,
their occupants having fled for the weekend.
Katherine decided that today she, too, deserved
to leave early. To hell with them all!

In the doorway of the library she paused. She
had hoped Sandra would be alone, but no, Stan
Herzberg was hovering at her desk, bending over
Sandra's blond head. His hand covered hers.

Stan was a company vice-president. He was
about forty-five, with dark, wavy hair streaked
with gray. He was quite good-looking, but Katherine had always thought there was something
rather unpleasant in his face. He wore a perpetual

slight tan (probably from the sunlamp at his health club), and his somewhat thickset body, encased today in a three-piece navy-blue suit that fit him flawlessly, was remarkably solid for a man his age.

He straightened the moment he saw Katherine. Caught off guard, he nodded to Sandra, saying, "Thank you for looking those figures up for me, Mrs. Jurgenson." He started away from her desk.

Katherine laughed. "Oh, come on now, Stan," she said mockingly. "You don't have to pretend in front of me. You were trying to put the make on Sandra!"

Stan drew himself up, his fingers tugging at the bottom of his vest, making the fabric taut. He regarded Katherine with narrowed eyes.

"Katherine!" Sandra said sharply. Katherine had gone too far this time—Stan was not the kind to mess with, certainly not openly like this. He had something of a reputation as a ladies' man, and one look could tell you he regarded himself as the answer to maidenly prayers. It was written all over him. But so what? Sandra enjoyed a bit of flirtation as well as the next girl, and if she had to, she could take care of him in her own way. Katherine's way would probably get them both fired. What the hell had gotten into her?

"Mr. Herzberg," Sandra said with a little smile, trying to appease him, "don't pay any attention to her. She's just kidding around."

"Sure she is," he said, staring poisonously at Katherine. Then he looked down, flicked his wrist and checked the time on a handsome Pulsar watch. "Well, it's four fifteen," he said. "I've got to be going. Have a good weekend, Mrs. Jurgenson," he said to Sandra. "Good-bye, Ms. Fielding."

Katherine laughed without pleasure and looked at Sandra, who was not smiling.

"Hey, I'm sorry about that," Katherine said sheepishly. "I don't know why I did it, but I was just so *pissed* when I came in here."

"Why?"

"Not only did I not get the promotion, but he gave the job to Bruce!"

"What!" Sandra's hand slapped her desk top. "Is that his idea of a joke?"

"Hilarious, isn't it?" Katherine said bitterly. "But at least he had the decency to be embarrassed when he told me."

"Well, he should! My God, Bruce is the laziest editor in the whole department. He spends half his time sitting in his office drunk."

"I know. Can you believe that I actually covered for him a few times?" Katherine sighed. "I can't blame him, though. He was offered the job and he took it. It's *Charles*." Katherine gritted her teeth as she said his name. "Christ! I hate him. And I hate this place. Look, let's just get out of here now. Okay?"

"Sure. Just give me a few minutes to put everything away."

"Fine. I'll get my coat and be right back." Katherine walked to the door and turned to add, "I don't know about you, but I feel like getting drunk tonight." Her eyes gleamed. "And *laid*. What do you say?"

Sandra looked at her. "Mmm, sure."

* * *

Charles was standing at the elevators. He was full of high spirits and looking forward to the weekend that was about to begin. He glanced up, surprised, as a sour-faced Stan Herzberg stalked toward him.

"Stan! Still here?" Charles said. "I thought you caught an earlier train on Fridays."

"Yeah, well, I missed it today," Stan grumbled.

"Anything wrong?"

"Nah, nothing really."

"So why the bad mood?"

Stan scowled. "I just had a little run-in with that Wasp princess you've got working in Editorial."

"Who? Katherine Fielding?" Charles laughed. "I guess I'm to blame for that. I turned her down for a promotion this afternoon, and when she left my office she was out for blood."

"Well, she sure picked on the wrong guy."

"She really got to you, didn't she? Well, I wouldn't pay too much attention to it, if I were you. She's kind of a hot-head, but she's just about the sharpest editor here."

"So why'd you turn her down?"

Charles shook his head. "Because she's too damn ambitious for her own good. If I didn't hold her back, she'd be after *my* job." He laughed. "You know, she's a funny one," Charles said as the elevator doors opened and they stepped in. "The first time I saw her—it must have been seven or eight years ago—I thought she was a model they sent up by mistake. I was all set to ask her out. She had long hair then and was wearing a miniskirt. Boy, did she have sensational legs!"

"Yeah, I remember that," Stan said. "But I haven't seen her in a short skirt in years. She's always wearing those damn long skirts or pants."

"Anyway," Charles continued, ignoring the interruption, "there she was with that beautiful face and all that long, dark hair, looking like she stepped out of *Vogue*. But did she set me straight right away! Whipped out her résumé and there were all those degrees and Phi Beta Kappa keys and whatnot. I hired her on the spot. But I never figured she'd be around long. You know who her father is, don't you?"

"Sure. Philip Fielding. Big Wall Street lawyer."

"As big as they come. That's why I thought she'd probably marry some Social Register guy and that would be that. She sure surprised me. But," he added confidentially, "I hear she doesn't get along too well with her father."

"I wonder why she's never gotten married," Stan mused.

The elevator opened and they stepped out into the lobby.

"I don't know," Charles said, "but you know she rooms with that blonde in the library. They're kind of an odd pair. You think they've got something going?"

"Nah," Stan said. "They're straight. Especially that blonde. She's not the type. Anyway, she's been married and divorced."

"Well, that doesn't always mean anything," Charles said. "But I suppose you're right. That blonde is kind of sexy, isn't she? She's got a nice little body on her. Great tits."

"Oh, yeah?" Stan said, trying to keep a straight face. "I've never noticed. I'll have to check that out."

"Jesus, where've you been? You must walk around the office with blinders on." Charles laughed and shook his head, sweeping the door open for Stan with a mock bow. "Hey, there's a cab," he said, and waved it over to the curb. "Got to run. Give my best to Louise and the kids."

"Will do," Stan said. He walked off in the direction of Grand Central Station.

All the way home to Mamaroneck he thought about Sandra Jurgenson: her soft, lovely face with those big, blue eyes, that sweet little body with those gorgeous breasts. He could almost feel them, swollen and straining in his grasp. Goddamn cockteaser. She was driving him crazy and he still wasn't sure whether she meant to let him score. Thinking about it, he regretted the afternoon's incident. Sandra was tight with that roommate of hers, and he had made a tactical error letting Queen Katherine throw him off like that. Come Monday, he would have to fix that.

At a table in the back of a bar where they were sure they wouldn't meet anyone from the company, Katherine tossed off one scotch on the rocks and quickly ordered another, while Sandra nursed a gin and tonic and waited for Katherine's anger to level off.

"Christ, I ought to go in there Monday morning and quit," Katherine muttered.

Sandra frowned at her. "Don't be an idiot. What good would that do?"

"It would make me feel better."

"Yeah, but what about me? I'm not paying the rent all by myself just so you can salvage your foolish pride."

Katherine looked at her. Money was not the problem, but Sandra had a point.

"Don't do anything outrageous," Sandra said. "Play it cool. Charles'll come around."

"Oh, no he won't."

"What makes you so sure?"

"Because he resents me, that's why. Because I'm a woman and I'm better educated than he is."

"*And* you come from an old Wasp family with lots of money and status."

Katherine looked at her coldly. "My family doesn't have anything to do with it."

"Okay, okay, I'm sorry I brought it up," Sandra said. She should have known better. Any mention of Katherine's family always elicited the same reaction: stone-cold silence. Her only idea of who they were came from a society-page photo she had happened to spot in the newspaper. Mr. and Mrs. Philip Fielding at some posh event or other. She often wondered why Katherine never talked about them. Her parents were sleek-looking people, the kind of people you'd think she'd be proud of. But she seemed ashamed of them instead. She stole a glance at her now, wondering what it was that was so mysterious in the Fielding family.

Katherine's anger seemed to have dissipated. She sat staring glumly into her drink. "Listen, forget about Charles," Sandra urged. "You need to relax, get your mind off things tonight. And I'm going to see to it that you do."

"How are you going to do that?" Katherine asked sullenly.

"Just leave that up to me," Sandra said. She put her hand on Katherine's arm and shook it gently. "But first of all, you've got to loosen up. You're too uptight and repressed. You've got to get rid of your inhibitions."

Katherine pulled away from her. She had heard this lecture before.

"Look at *me*," Sandra said. "Before I got divorced I was even more inhibited than you are. I was twenty-five and I was acting like a goddamn Minneapolis *matron*. But I dumped that tight-assed Viking I was married to and I split. Since then I've been open to every new experience."

"That's for sure."

"Cut the sarcasm. I'm serious, Katherine. I'm a different person than I was two years ago when I came to New York. I'm freer, *happier*. And it's all because I overcame my stupid middle-class hang-ups."

"Well, *I* don't think I'm so inhibited. I like getting laid, too. And wasn't I the one to suggest that we go out cruising tonight?"

"Sure, but that's not what I mean. You're too uptight. You never want to try anything new."

"Maybe you're right," Katherine glowered, "but stop *pushing* me."

"All right," Sandra relented. "I guess my timing could be better. Forget it for now. Let's just go out and have a good time tonight. You deserve it."

## CHAPTER TWO

They worked their way uptown, moving from bar to bar. It was a technique they used whenever they went out to pick up men. If they found slim pickings in one place, they'd move on to another. Usually the system worked and they met someone who interested them—at least for a night. And when it didn't work, they just kept moving north on First Avenue until they were home.

By the time they reached Ziggy's, a neighborhood hangout in the low Seventies, they were both slightly drunk.

The place was noisy and dark. They grabbed a table that had just been vacated, and as they sat down, a couple of men smiled at them from the crowded bar several feet away. Katherine, angling her chair away, pretended not to notice. Sandra flashed a disdainful look that said, *Forget it.*

They ordered drinks, and then Katherine made a survey of the room. "Now I know why we don't come in here more often," she said. "These guys are all creeps."

As the drinks came, a man pushed his way

through the crowd at the bar and sauntered over to their table. He was in his late thirties and dressed in a figured body shirt open to the waist and a pair of tight, faded jeans. Around his neck were a number of gold chains and necklaces. The two women ignored him.

He bent down and looked intently at Katherine. "My God, you've got beautiful eyes," he said. "They're the kind of eyes that could hypnotize a man. I bet you're a witch."

"I'm not interested," Katherine said coldly. "Please go away."

"No. No, I can't. I'm under your spell. You've enchanted me," the man said, clasping his hand to his heart to show he was in her thrall.

Katherine glanced at Sandra for help, but Sandra was staring into her drink, having no part of it.

"Look, I don't care what I've done to you. Just get out of here!" she went on with real annoyance.

"I won't leave until you tell me who you are, oh, beautiful Witch of the East." He folded his hands before him in a mock plaintive gesture.

"Jesus! I guess we'll just have to leave this place! Let's go, Sandra." Katherine grabbed Sandra's arm and began shaking it. "Let's go!"

"Excuse me," a voice said, "but you seem to be bothering my wife and sister." A tall, attractive man had stepped up to the table, and both women looked up at him.

The first man sized his opponent up and quickly recovered from his enchantment. "Oh, hey, man, I'm sorry. I didn't mean to intrude," he said and scuttled away.

Katherine and Sandra sighed with relief and the handsome stranger smiled at them.

"I wish I *had* enchanted him," Katherine said. "I would have turned him into a toad—except he already looks like one."

The man laughed. "I've seen him around before," he said. "He always pulls that 'witchcraft' line. Believe it or not, it sometimes works."

"Well, he's not my type," Katherine said. "Anyway, thanks for helping out. Can we show you our gratitude by buying you a drink?"

"Women's liberation, I love it!" He pulled up a chair. "You're on. But only if you'll let me buy the next round."

"Sure." The two women exchanged glances that acknowledged that this man was interesting.

"My name's Ted Hanley," he told them. "What's yours?"

Katherine and Sandra introduced themselves.

He appeared to be in his mid-thirties. He had thick, dark hair and wore tortoise-shell glasses that gave him a slightly bookish air. He was dressed in a gray turtleneck and jeans. When he had ordered his drink he said, "I don't think I've seen you two in here before. Do you live around here?"

"Not too far," Katherine answered.

"At Eighty-fifth and First," Sandra volunteered, ignoring Katherine's evasiveness. "We're roommates—and we also work at the same place."

"And what place is that?"

"Roth Publishing," Sandra answered. "Katherine's an editor on *Trend* magazine, and I run the library there."

"Oh, really?" he said. "I read *Trend*—it's usually got some good articles in it. But I can't say that I like your film critic. He's almost as bad as John Simon."

"But you still read him," Katherine said. "And that's the point."

"Yes," he said. "I suppose it is."

Katherine had been quietly appraising Ted Hanley from the moment he sat down. She liked what she saw. He didn't quite fit the whole singles' bar scene. He wasn't laden with a tacky assortment of male jewelry—but only wore a watch, and her expert eye told her it was the real thing, a Cartier's tank watch. Nice, she thought. "What do you do?" Katherine asked him.

"I'm an account executive with Preswick, Knight," he said.

"What accounts do you handle?" Sandra asked, impressed. Preswick, Knight was an important advertising agency, almost as big as BBD&O.

"Whatever I can get." He flashed a somewhat cynical smile and took a long pull on his drink. "But I'd rather not talk about advertising tonight. I'd rather talk about you two." He leaned toward Sandra. "Now, you. I know you're not from New York, right?"

"Right you are," Sandra said. "I'm just a country girl."

"Hey, come on." He smiled. "That twang of yours is nice." He lit a cigarette and grinned at Sandra. "So, tell me about yourself," he urged.

"Oh, there's not much to tell," Sandra said. "I was born and raised near Minneapolis and went to the university there." She took a breath and went on. "I got married right after college, taught for a while, and then my husband wanted to have a baby. I didn't, and we fought over it." Her voice had taken on a sing-song quality, as if she had repeated this story dozens of times. "Finally, I divorced him and came to New York. That was about two years ago," she concluded.

"Why did you want to leave the Land of Ten Thousand Lakes?" he asked.

Sandra smiled sardonically. "The divorce wasn't too popular on the homefront. My parents —my mother especially—just didn't understand it. I think she would have gladly drowned me in one of those lakes. It seemed like a good idea to get out of town."

He nodded. "What made you pick New York?"

"Oh, I don't know," Sandra said. "It just seemed like the right place to go after a divorce."

"Yeah, I guess so," he said, "although I wouldn't know personally. I've never been divorced—or married either, for that matter."

He looked at Katherine. "What about you?" he said. "Ever been married?"

She curled her lip and shook her head, but he barely paused for her answer; he was too preoccupied with what he was going to say to her next. "You don't seem to want to talk about yourself like your friend here," he said. "What's the matter? Something to hide?"

Katherine stiffened. "I don't think that's any of your business," she said haughtily.

Ted seemed slightly uncomfortable. "Look, I didn't mean to pry," he said to Katherine. "I was just trying to get to know you."

Katherine studied his face a moment and then relaxed. He had seemed almost genuine to her in that moment—and yet for all his earnestness, there was something cold, something she didn't trust about him. Maybe it was his eyes—that ardent look that proclaimed *I'm sincere*, even as he scanned their faces, measuring the impression he was making. Their eyes met briefly. Katherine turned away, and a silent, awkward moment passed before Sandra made an attempt to revive the conversation on a lighter note.

"Do you come here very often?" she asked Ted.

"Oh, off and on," he said. "I don't hang out in here, if that's what you mean. The crowd gets to me sometimes." He jerked his head in the direction of the next table, where three young women were covertly eying the men at the bar under cover of a loud, too animated conversation. "What dogs," he said snidely. "The girls you meet in here are usually like that."

"And are we different?" Sandra asked.

"Hell, yes. You two are *very* foxy." He glanced at Katherine. "You're obviously bright—I mean, you don't look like file clerks—and you don't seem on the prowl for whatever you can pick up."

"No?" Katherine said. "How can you be sure?"

He hesitated a moment, uncertain whether she was being sarcastic or not. Then he smiled knowingly, a little smugly, she thought. "Oh, I saw a few guys give you the eye from the bar," he said, "but you turned up your noses at them. And you weren't at all interested in the Toad."

Katherine laughed. "Did it occur to you that we might be lesbians?"

He raised his eyebrows. "Not you two. You looked like you were only interested in quality stuff. Most of the girls who come in here dump their girlfriends for the first guy who smiles at them."

"No, we're cool," Sandra said with a grin. "We waited for the second one."

Hanley chuckled, then suddenly turned serious. "By the way," he said, appraising first Sandra then Katherine, "are you both the same age?"

"No," Sandra said, surprised at the question. She looked over at Katherine. "I'm twenty-seven."

"And I'm thirty," Katherine added.

"No kidding. So am I," Ted said.

Katherine mused that he was still attractive, but clearly older than that. She wondered why he would ask the question in the first place, and then lie about such a silly thing. She was about to query him when he abruptly turned and called the waitress over to the table. "Give us another round," he said.

"Not for me," Katherine said. "I'm not finished with this one."

"Neither am I," Sandra said.

"Then you'd better drink up, ladies!" He laughed. "Get us that round," he said to the waitress. "After all, don't forget," he said when she was gone, "this one is on me."

"Don't worry," Katherine said. "We won't leave you out when it comes time for the final reckoning."

"Good," he said. "Because I don't like to mooch off women." There was a trace of defensiveness in his tone.

Katherine looked askance at him. "Oh, come on, now," she said. "Do women regularly try to keep you?"

"Well, a woman has, at least once, for your information," he asserted. "But that's a heavy story."

"Oh, *do* tell us."

Ted shrugged his shoulders. "Okay, but remember, you asked for it," he said and smiled broadly. "Well," he began, "when I was a lot younger I thought I wanted to be an actor, and I was studying with this acting group. There was this older woman there who was very rich and she came to the group just to meet guys like me. She was about fifty, but really well preserved. One day, she asked me over to her apartment to 'read' with her. Of course, I knew what she wanted. And I was right." His smile was smug. "When I got there she forgot all about the reading and seduced me instead. Well, you know the rest. She bought me a lot of stuff and had me move in with her for a while. That lasted for a couple of months, and then I guess she just got tired of me. But boy," he laughed, "I sure learned a lot from her. She turned me on to lots of things." He paused dramatically. "I guess you could say she changed my life."

"In what way?" Katherine asked.

"Well, for one thing, she made me realize just how much I liked the finer things in life, and so I decided to give up acting and concentrate on a more lucrative career. But there were other things she taught me, too—sexual things." He looked at them expectantly.

Sandra took the bait. She leaned toward Ted. "What kind of sexual things?"

"Ho, ho. What's this?" he said, his eyes flashing. "Midwesterners are supposed to be uptight about sex, aren't they?"

"Some are and some aren't," Sandra said with a slow, sultry smile.

"And I can see which side you're on." He grinned back at her.

"Well, come on, tell us," Katherine said, more interested in his story than the games he was playing with Sandra. "What did she teach you?"

Ted laughed. "I sure know how to pick 'em, don't I? I knew you two were a couple of live ones the first time I laid eyes on you!" He grabbed both their hands and squeezed them. "Hey, you're really all right," he said. He seemed to be enjoying himself immensely.

Then he withdrew his hands and sat back in his chair. "Well," he went on with mock confidentiality, "about my sexual education. My most interesting lesson was in *ménage à trois*. The old gal had this maid, kind of young but not too pretty, and every once in a while she'd call the maid into the bedroom when we were making it, and then the maid would join in and she'd make it with me and then the old lady." He shook his head. "But I never could understand how that maid could get up out of bed and go back to her chores as if nothing had happened. *That* was really strange."

"Some people will do anything for money," Katherine offered ironically. Including him, obviously, she thought. He was driving at something with this little tale, but she wasn't sure what it was.

"Yeah," Ted said. Once again, he hardly seemed to have heard her, but was calculating the impact he'd made. "Well, what about you two? Shocked?" he said. "You girls would never get together with just one guy. Right, ladies?"

Katherine looked down at her drink. God, is he ever transparent, she thought.

But Sandra smiled at him. "Could be," she teased.

"Oh, so you're not quite so innocent as you look?" he inquired.

"*I'm* not so innocent as I look," Sandra said. "I don't think Katherine looks very innocent, do you? She's much more sophisticated."

"Yeah, but a lot of very sophisticated-looking ladies are really uptight about sex. What about it?" he said to Katherine.

"Let's just say that I've managed to overcome a lot of my hangups on that subject," she said stiffly.

"Well, good!" he said and raised his glass. "A toast to overcoming hangups!" They clinked glasses with him and drank. "Hey, another round," he said, gesturing the waitress over to their table. "I insist. You see," he said, ordering the round, "it's a celebration."

"What's the occasion?" Sandra asked.

"Finding two such sexy, intelligent creatures as you." He laughed insinuatingly. "That doesn't happen to me every day."

"It's your reward for rescuing us," Sandra said.

"Oh, yeah, that's right," Ted said thoughtfully. "I did do a good deed this evening, didn't I?"

"You see," Katherine said, "there's still something to be said for chivalry."

Suddenly he looked at them both with a greater intensity. "So, are you two my reward?"

"It depends on what you have in mind," Sandra said coyly.

Katherine tried to signal Sandra with her eyes, but couldn't catch her gaze. So, giving a little moan, she put her hand to her head. "Hey, I feel a little dizzy," she said.

"Are you going to be sick?" Sandra asked. "If you are, let me take you to the ladies' room."

Covering her mouth with her hand, Katherine nodded weakly.

Ted shot Sandra a look of annoyance. "You'd better get her out of here," he said.

"Okay," Sandra said, getting up. She walked around the table and helped Katherine out of her chair. "We'll be right back," she said over her shoulder to Ted. "Don't go away."

He flashed her a smile. "I'll be here."

His eyes followed them as they walked to the back of the room, and lingered on Sandra's well-rounded ass in her skintight pants.

The ladies' room was crowded and they had to get in line. Katherine turned to Sandra. "It's okay. I'm not sick," she said, "although I have had too much to drink. What do you want to do about him?"

"I don't know," Sandra said. "I like him, though.

And it's rather obvious that he wants to make it with both of us."

"Yeah," Katherine agreed. Then she frowned. "But I'm not so sure. There's something about him. . . . I don't know. Do you get any funny feeling about him?"

"Like what?"

"Well, he's been around. He didn't just tell us that story about the older woman by accident."

"I realize that."

"Well, I just think he's a lot more calculating than he pretends."

"Does that turn you off?"

Katherine shook her head. "No, it's not that," she said. "We've met worse creeps. But why does he want to make it with both of us?"

"Oh, come on, Katherine. All men have fantasies like that."

"Yeah, sure. But he's so obvious about it."

"So? You can't blame him for trying."

"No. I guess not. But I've never done anything like that."

"You know what they say. There's always a first time for everything."

"I knew you'd say that. Maybe I'd just better go home and you can go with him."

"If you go, I go."

"Dammit, Sandra, don't do that to me! I don't want to spoil your fun."

"Then why don't you come along? Look, if you're uncomfortable we'll just go home."

"Wouldn't that be a little awkward?"

"What do you care? If you don't like it, let me know and we'll leave."

Katherine fell silent. She was thinking about what Sandra had said earlier about her being too inhibited. Maybe that was true. But she wasn't always that way, was she? Like tonight. She really had felt like doing something outrageous. And this guy's smugness kind of turned her on, made her want to show him. And as long as things didn't get too kinky everything would be all right. So, what the hell. Even though she'd probably regret it tomorrow, why not enjoy tonight? "Okay," she said finally. "You talked me into it."

"Great," Sandra said. "At least with this guy there seems to be a little something else going on. Most of these clowns are so overeager they practically jump you in the bar."

Katherine laughed and then winced as if she were in pain. "I shouldn't laugh," she said, "or I think my bladder will burst. Let me go first, will you?" She pointed to an empty stall.

"Okay. But make it fast."

"What took you so long?" Ted asked sharply. He jerked the swizzle stick he had been chewing on out of his mouth and threw it on the table.

Katherine covered her irritation with a smile. "Sorry," she said. "I'm feeling better now, but what I really need is some fresh air."

"Do you want to go home?" Ted asked her. Katherine shook her head. He grinned. "Then how about the two of you coming over to my place? It's just a few blocks from here."

## CHAPTER THREE

He steered them up First Avenue. They walked slowly, arm in arm, occasionally bumping into passers-by because they took up so much space on the sidewalk and none of them was exactly steady on his feet. At the corner of Seventy-seventh Street, Ted steered them left and led them to a small, old-fashioned apartment building in the middle of the block. There was no elevator, so they climbed the stairs and he let them into his second-floor apartment and turned on the lights.

"Wow!" Sandra said as she gazed around the living room. "It's like being in one of Bloomingdale's designer rooms!"

It was a man's apartment, done in shades of brown. One wall was exposed brick, and in the middle of it was a wood-burning fireplace. Facing it was a large, dark-brown suede couch. In one corner was an Eames chair and in another corner stood a tall, chrome étagère with a few books, plants, stereo components and small pieces of sculpture artfully arranged on it. A large free-form copper sculpture graced a tortoise-shell parson's table just to the right of the door. There was another low parson's table in front of the couch. On the walls were a number of graphics—all of them in shades of brown, rust or orange. A tweedy-brown carpet covered the floor, and the windows were encased in thick, beige drapes. Not one thing was out of place, as if no one really lived there.

Katherine appraised the graphics with a critical eye. They could have been done by a machine. She was sure that they had been chosen solely to match the color scheme. Then she looked at the copper sculpture and shuddered inwardly. It was the ugliest thing she had ever seen.

Her reaction went unnoticed. Ted was too pleased with the impression the room had made on Sandra. "Well, it's not quite that great," he said, meaning that it was. "And," he confessed, "I did have some help with it from a designer friend of my roommate's."

"You've got a roommate?" Katherine asked. She was surprised; he didn't seem the type.

"Yeah," Ted shrugged. "The poor guy had a messy, expensive divorce so I let him move in with me. He's not around much, though. Right now, he's away for the weekend."

He took their coats and asked them if they wanted a drink.

"Not me," Sandra responded.

"I think I've had enough already," Katherine said.

"Then why don't you sit down"—he gestured toward the couch—"and I'll put on a little music."

He picked out a record and placed it on the turntable.

"Oh, Shostakovich," Katherine said as the opening chords of a symphony blared into the room. "He's one of my favorites."

"Mmm," Ted said, stealing a glance at the album jacket. He took off his glasses and sat down on the couch between them. "I would have thought Bach was more your style."

"Why is that?" Katherine asked. Who is he trying to kid? she thought. I'll bet he doesn't know Bach from the Beach Boys.

"Because you seem so controlled, so measured," he said, taking a shot in the dark. He slipped his arm around her. "Are you?"

"Not all the time," she said, leaning against him. His body was warm and firm and he smelled expensive.

He turned his attention to Sandra. "And you," he said. "I'll bet you were Homecoming Queen in high school." His other arm went around her with a playful squeeze.

She shook her head. "Runner-up," she admitted, throwing her arms around him.

He smiled at her and then leaned down and gave her a long kiss. Tentatively, Katherine pulled down the neck of his sweater and kissed the side of his throat. He smiled and began to hum, "Double your pleasure, double your fun." In spite of herself, Katherine had to laugh, and as he turned to kiss her, Sandra slipped her hands under his sweater and caressed his waist and taut abdomen. "Let's go into the bedroom," he said brusquely.

He led them down a short hall and threw open the door to a room done in stark black and white, a jarring contrast to the deep, earthy tones of the living room. The king-size bed was covered with a black spread and red and white pillows, reflected in a huge mirror on the wall behind it. On the floor was a large, white flokati rug, and there was a tall, white formica dresser in one corner, along with a desk of the same material. A huge color TV dominated another corner. There were several black-and-white photographs on the walls —all of them of nude women.

"Is that the bathroom?" Katherine pointed to a door in the corner. He nodded. "Well, then I think I'll use it," she said. "I've got to make a few preparations." She carried her purse with her into the bathroom and closed the door.

He was pulling the pillows off the bed. "Give me a hand with these, will you?"

Sandra picked up a couple of pillows and tossed them to the floor beside the bed. Then she helped him pull back the spread and a white wool blanket, exposing red satin sheets. They shimmered scarlet in the mirror behind. "Jesus," she said, "you don't believe in being subtle, do you?"

"Not where it counts, baby," Ted said, his glance taking in Sandra's amusement and the startled look of Katherine, who had emerged from the bathroom and was leaning against the dresser.

He sat down on the edge of the bed. "Come here, you two," he beckoned. "Undress me."

They obliged him, Katherine hesitating, then moving forward, suppressing her irritation. But his macho manner disappeared and he was suddenly passive as they took off his clothes. Katherine liked him much better that way.

Naked, he lay back on the bed. He had a beautiful body—lean and well-muscled. As he arched his back and ran his hand lovingly along his thigh, he smiled up at them. "Okay," he said, "it's your turn."

They stood in the middle of the room. Katherine took off her boots and, turning away from Ted's gaze, removed her slacks and placed them, neatly folded, on a chair. Sandra smiled boldly at him, pulled her sweater over her head and tossed it in the direction of the chair. Ted's eyes were riveted on her breasts. Her erect nipples were visible through the filmy cloth of her bra. She reached behind her and unhooked the bra, watching his face, his widening eyes, as he saw her large, naked breasts fall free. His lips parted slightly. "Oh, baby," he moaned, "bring those to me."

"Not yet," Sandra teased. She glanced over at Katherine. "You'll get us both together."

Katherine avoided Sandra's eyes. She had pulled off her sweater and was fumbling with the buttons on her blouse.

Sandra continued undressing with slow, seductive motions, flirting with Ted, while out of the corner of her eye she watched Katherine disrobe. Caressing herself as she peeled her slacks and panties from her body, she contemplated Katherine's long, tapered legs, her slender hips and waist, the perfect cone-shaped breasts. She longed to have a body like Katherine's instead of her own short, dumpy one. She knew that men liked her opulent curves, but she herself would have gladly traded her voluptuousness for Katherine's sleek, slim grace.

"Come on, come on," Ted was saying, "get your asses over here."

Katherine's temper flared, but before she could speak, Sandra jumped in. "Hey, lover boy," she said coolly. "You're not going to get anywhere with us talking like that."

"Okay, okay," Ted relented. "But you're driving me crazy standing there." His eyes flicked back and forth over their bodies. "Come over here. *Please.*"

"That's better," Sandra said. She moved to the bed and positioned herself next to him. Ted put an arm around her and then motioned to Katherine, who was still standing in the middle of the room. "You, too," he said, patting the bed on the other side. Slowly, Katherine approached the bed and lay down where he had indicated. Then, his arm was around her, his mouth on hers, in a grinding, passionate kiss. The thrill she felt surprised her.

Sandra snuggled closer, raising herself slightly to press her breasts against his chest, and nuzzled his neck. Releasing Katherine, Ted turned to kiss Sandra, while Katherine curled herself against the length of his back, caressing his buttocks with her hand.

Ted's fingers found Sandra's breasts, exploring, kneading, rubbing, harder and harder, until she closed her eyes and let her head drop back, surrendering to sensation. Katherine's hand strayed from Ted's buttocks to his stomach, touching it lightly. Suddenly he seized it and placed it on his erect penis.

Instinctively, Katherine began to pull away. But his hand was covering hers, pressing it against him, forcing her to feel the hardness, the warmth of his penis, and, excited now, she began stroking him. She twined her legs through his.

Intertwined, they began moving together rhythmically. Katherine, rubbing her body against Ted's back, was aware of Sandra's flesh touching hers—the soft thighs touching her own, fingertips grazing her hip—but she was beyond caring.

Ted was writhing and groaning with pleasure, and soon his smooth, almost hairless body was glistening with a thin film of sweat that made his muscles stand out in sharp definition. Katherine fantasized that he was a Greek statue come to life, perfectly proportioned and beautifully muscled.

His hands clutched wildly at them, massaging their buttocks and breasts, and he arched his back as the two women strained their bodies against his. Sandra let her lips roam over his chest to his nipples, flicking them with her tongue, nibbling at them. Katherine twisted her body around as she kissed the flat expanse of his stomach, the soft hollow of his groin, working her way downward toward his penis, while she continued to stroke it frantically with her hand.

She had her mouth around the tip when Ted gave her head an abrupt push. She started to gag but he held her head down. When she tried to lift it he only pushed harder and rammed his penis deeper into her mouth. Choking now, she reached up and wrenched his hand away. She started to move away from him but he grabbed her arm roughly.

"Get on top of me," he said hoarsely.

Briefly, she was torn between her fury and her mounting excitement. Her ardor won. She straddled him, and he shoved his penis inside her.

Through half-closed eyes, Sandra watched them thrusting at each other. Ted was sucking on her breasts but it was the expression on Katherine's face that fascinated her. Katherine's eyes were squeezed shut but her mouth was open and she was breathing heavily. Sandra could have reached out her hand and touched her.

Within moments Ted's whole body stiffened and he began to make little grunting noises. Then it was over and he lay completely still, but Katherine continued to move, faster, more urgently until, suddenly her eyes opened and she stopped. Without looking at either of them, she pulled away from him and lay down on the far side of the bed.

Ted brushed the beads of sweat from his forehead and then grinned up at Sandra. "Just let me recharge my batteries, baby," he said, "and I'll give it to you, too."

Sandra raised an eyebrow.

"Hell, I can go ten times in one night without even breathing hard," he blustered.

"That I'd like to see," Sandra said.

"Maybe you will—if you're good," Ted said. "Go get me a cigarette now, and then I'll let you get me hard again."

Sandra got up and went to the dresser. She got a cigarette, lit it and brought it back to him, handing him an ashtray from the nightstand.

He smoked in silence for several minutes. Then he glanced over at Katherine.

"I think your friend here is asleep," he said to Sandra.

Katherine's eyes stayed closed, but she shook her head. "No, I'm not. I'm just resting."

Ted smiled smugly. "Well, as soon as I'm finished with Blondie here," he said to Katherine, "she'll need a rest too."

Katherine's eyes flew open. She stared at him, but he was busy putting his cigarette out.

"Okay, babe," he said to Sandra. "Let's fuck."

He began pawing at Sandra's breasts and she responded by kneading his penis. Within a few minutes he had another erection and he was on top of her.

Katherine turned away from them. She felt angry and degraded. Ted might have a gorgeous body, but he was a pig. The great lover couldn't even make her come. And now she had to lie here and listen to them humping away at each other. No more threesomes. Never again. She wanted to go home.

When Ted and Sandra separated and lay back side by side, Katherine kept her back to them. No one said a word. Five minutes passed. Then suddenly Ted slid off the bed, got a cigarette and lit it, and walked back to the foot of the bed.

"Okay," he said, exhaling dramatically, "now, why don't you two make it with each other?"

Katherine turned and looked at him sharply. "What?"

"Don't play dumb," Ted said. "You heard me."

"Yes, I heard you," Katherine said, sitting up. "I just couldn't believe my ears."

"Oh, come on," he goaded. "Don't tell me you've never done it."

Katherine's jaw tightened, but Sandra sat up quickly and put a restraining hand on Katherine's arm. "No, we haven't," Sandra said in a conciliatory voice.

"So?" He shrugged. "Do it anyway. You'll probably get off on it."

Katherine shook off Sandra's hand. "Look," she snapped, "I'm getting sick and tired of your ordering us around!"

"Sooo," he said, pressing his lips together. "You want me to get tough with you!" He laughed, a strange, hollow laugh. "Yeah, that's the way you bitches are. You like it when a guy gets a little mean. And I'm just the guy to do it to you!"

Sandra flashed an urgent look at Katherine. She was ready to grab her clothes and run, but Katherine was incensed—no man was going to try and push her around like that and get away with it.

"Look," Katherine said again, getting up, "we don't want any part of you. We're leaving!"

"You cunt!" He took a step toward her. "Who do you think you are? Some high-class piece of ass? You can get away with that with some guys, baby, but not with me. No broad calls the shots with me!"

"Fuck you!"

"Katherine! Stop it!" Sandra said. "Let's just go."

"Sure," Katherine turned to say to her, "we'll get out of here, but first I want to tell this dumb shit where to get off!"

"You're not going anywhere," he said. "Not until you do what I want." He positioned himself between them and the door, his legs planted in a defiant stance.

Sandra had started to get up from the bed, and now she slowly sank back down on it. But Katherine whirled, facing him.

"You son of a bitch!" she said. "Let us out of here!"

He shook his head. "Not a chance."

"All right, you mother-fucking bastard!" She was shouting now and close to tears. "But you can't *force* us to do what you want!"

A muscle twitched in his face and he fixed her with a cold, blank stare. "Oh, I think I can," he said. He backed toward the closet, never taking his eyes from them as he reached inside. He pulled out a thick, black leather belt with a large, heavy brass buckle, and began methodically to coil its length around his right fist.

"Oh, my God," Sandra moaned.

He tapped the buckle against the palm of his other hand and leered at Sandra. "You'd like this, baby, wouldn't you?" He began advancing on the bed, hitting his palm harder and harder with each step.

Sandra scrambled back against the mirrored wall, at the head of the bed. As her shoulder grazed the cold glass, she turned away with a shudder, and her eyes fastened briefly on the telephone on the nightstand.

Ted caught her look. "I wouldn't try that," he said. He was at the foot of the bed now. "Who're you going to call? The cops?" He laughed mirthlessly.

Katherine hadn't moved. She was standing just behind him and a little to the side. Her eyes were vacant and seemed to be riveted on a spot on the far wall.

Ted flipped the belt teasingly at Sandra. "Come on, baby," he said, "you want me to hurt you, don't you?"

Sandra began whimpering with fear. There were no pillows on the bed, nothing to protect her. She cowered against the mirrored wall, covering her face with her hands. Every time the belt hit the bed it was coming closer. Then it hit her, hard across the ass and thigh. She recoiled from the impact and cried out in pain.

He drew back the belt to hit her again, and Sandra put out her hand to ward off the blow. The buckle bit through the skin on the back of her hand. She screamed.

The outcry made Katherine jump. She turned her head and watched, horrified, as the belt went flying through the air again and again, the buckle glimmering as it swept in an arc, leaping dangerously close to the panel of glass. Sandra's flesh quivered as it struck her, and then blossomed with ugly red welts. Her body twisted and squirmed to avoid the increasing fury of the blows. But there was no escape.

"You little slut," he growled. "You love it. I

know you do!" The belt flashed through the air faster now, harder, missing Sandra narrowly, then pounding at her again.

Then Katherine caught sight of Ted's face in the mirror. His eyes had narrowed to slits and his lips were drawn back from his teeth in a fiendish grin. Katherine gasped. This was not happening; it could not be real. But the red welts on Sandra's body were real and her screams were piercing the air.

No! He's got to stop. *I've got to do something,* Katherine thought, panicking. But what? If she grabbed for the belt, he would turn it on her. She did not dare fight him, he was too strong. She needed a weapon, something to make him drop the belt. Frantically, her eyes darted around the room and seized on an object glinting on the desk top a few feet away. A long, slender sterling silver letter opener.

Again the belt lashed out at Sandra. She was wailing now, screaming and crying, squirming with pain and fear. Intent on Sandra's writhing agony, Ted seemed oblivious of Katherine standing frozen in horror and indecision behind him.

He had his back to her and was lifting his arm to swing the belt at Sandra again when Katherine grabbed the letter opener and lunged at him. He had reached forward and was about to bring the buckle down on Sandra's thigh. Suddenly, he twisted his body to the right and Katherine was over him, driving the point into his back just below the left shoulder, pushing it down, deeper, deeper, until she could feel damp flesh pressing up against her fist. For a moment his dazed eyes caught hers in the mirror. Then he gasped loudly and collapsed across the bed, hands clutching wildly at the satin sheet, legs sliding down over the edge. The belt had fallen to the floor. His body shuddered convulsively and then was completely still, and there was blood everywhere. It flowed onto the sheets, oozing black against the scarlet satin, and spread a red stain on the white blanket and onto the white rug. Katherine had fallen with him, still clutching the letter opener; she pulled it out. Blood spurted up at her in a fountain, soaking her. Her hand and arm were covered with it.

Neither of the women said a word. They stared at the hole in Ted Hanley's back and the blood gushing out of it.

Slowly Sandra looked up at Katherine. She was still standing over him, as if waiting for him to get up. He didn't move.

"Katherine!" Sandra whispered. "Is he dead?" She knew he was.

Katherine's eyes were glazed. She was staring at the body, but she couldn't seem to focus on it.

Then she started to cry. Sandra strained to look at Katherine. It was hard to take it all in, and there was so much blood on her that Sandra thought at first that Katherine might have been cut herself. She moved to the edge of the bed and tried to stand up, but she was so weak from the fright of the beating that her legs shook when she put her weight on them. She walked haltingly over to Katherine and put her arm around her.

"It's all right, it's all right," she soothed. Katherine shook her violently away and began sobbing uncontrollably. It wasn't all right, it would never be all right again.

"No," Sandra said. "You're right. It's *not* all right." She sighed and looked down at Katherine's body. Her breasts were smeared with thick, dark blood; her stomach, her thighs were splattered with it.

"Are you hurt?" Sandra asked.

Katherine opened her eyes and looked at her blankly and then slowly bent her head to look at her body. A little sob escaped from her mouth and she sagged against Sandra.

Instinctively, Sandra's free hand reached out to support Katherine's body, and her fingers slid across some blood. It was still slightly warm.

Sandra held her for several minutes until Katherine's sobs abated. Then she said gently, "Why don't you go and wash that stuff off?"

Katherine moved like a sleepwalker through the bathroom door, and Sandra shoved aside the things on the chair and sat down. She was vaguely aware of the throbbing ache in her backside, her thighs and arms—everywhere the buckle had found flesh. But she pushed the pain out of her mind. She needed to think.

The blood was beginning to dry on her hand where she had touched Katherine. By separating her fingers she could feel how sticky it was—like strawberry jam. Her eyes were drawn to the body on the bed. There was so much more blood there, so red and dark. And everything was so still. Yet, it was hard to realize that he was dead. She could almost imagine the scene running backward, like trick photography: the blood going back into his body, the wound sealing up, Ted himself getting up, picking up the belt, turning toward her. . . .

She drew her breath in sharply. For a moment she had seen him again, looming over her, grinning, bringing the belt down. She shook herself, and her eyes sought out the wound in his back. She stared at it, transfixed, and felt a small, shuddery feeling stir in the pit of her stomach. All that blood. And he had deserved it. Deserved to die. It was beautiful and just. For a fleeting moment she imagined she had done it herself. Her eyes squeezed shut, she could see herself raising the letter opener, plunging it in. Deeper, deeper, harder. . . . The shuddery feeling swelled within her. Repressing it, she opened her eyes and was suddenly aware of the utter stillness around her. Absolute silence. No sound of running water from the bathroom. Nothing.

She got up and walked into the bathroom.

Katherine was standing motionless, staring at her bloody image in the mirror. Her face was streaked with tears.

Tenderly, Sandra touched her arm. "Katherine, come on. I'll wash you off."

Katherine let herself be led into the shower stall. Sandra turned the shower on and directed the nozzle at Katherine's body. The blood coursed down her legs in thin streams.

"There, you see? It's all coming off," she said softly.

"No!" Katherine cried. "Get it off me. Get it off!"

"Shhh, it's okay," Sandra said, trying to calm

her. "I'll take care of it." She picked up the soap
and a washcloth hanging over the door. She lath-
ered the soap and carefully began to wash Katherine's body, passing the cloth lightly over her.
Shoulders, back, belly.

"Make it hotter," Katherine insisted.

Clouds of steam were already filling the stall,
but Sandra adjusted the water. Almost scalding
now, the heat stung the welts on her hip, but she
ignored the pain and concentrated on Katherine.

Where the blood had begun to coagulate, she
had to rub harder to get it off, but Katherine stood
passively, seeming to welcome the pressure as
Sandra scrubbed back and forth over her chest.
The cloth grazed her breasts, raising her nipples.
For a moment Sandra was tempted to touch
them, touch the hard, firm flesh, flushed from the
friction of the cloth. Quickly, she picked up Katherine's right arm. The letter opener was still
clutched in her hand. Sandra attempted to pry it
free, but Katherine's grasp was too tight. Slowly,
one by one, Sandra uncurled the fingers. The letter opener clattered to the floor of the shower
stall.

She washed Katherine's hand and arm, survey-
ing the rest of her body to see if she had missed
any spot. Just to make sure, she bent down and
painstakingly washed off Katherine's legs and
feet.

"There. It's all off," Sandra said, turning off
the water. "You're clean."

Katherine nodded listlessly.

Sandra stepped away from the shower stall and
got a towel, briskly drying herself then draping

the damp towel around Katherine's shoulders. Taking another towel from the rack, she dropped to her knees and began slowly, gently, patting Katherine dry.

"Do you think you can get dressed by yourself?" she asked.

"Uh-huh," Katherine said and walked out of the bathroom. She went to the chair in the bedroom, picked up her clothes and mechanically began putting them on. Sandra followed her out of the bathroom and started dressing herself. As Katherine was stepping into her pants, she staggered, and Sandra rushed to catch her before she fell.

"What are you doing?" Katherine said sharply. "I can take care of myself."

"Fine," Sandra said and let go of Katherine's arm.

Katherine finished dressing and sat down on the chair, out of the sight line of the corpse on the bed. "Are the police coming?" she asked.

Sandra looked at her for several long seconds. "No," she said. "I didn't call them."

Katherine's head jerked up. "Why not?"

"I've been thinking," Sandra said. "Maybe we don't have to call them."

Katherine looked at her uncertainly.

"We'd be taking a risk, I know," Sandra went on, "but it's risky if we *do* call the police. It was an accident, but the situation doesn't look very good for us, does it?"

Katherine dropped her head limply. "No."

"And you know what they'd do to you," Sandra added. "Because of your family I mean—"

"Don't say any more," Katherine blurted out. "You've made your point."

Sandra took a deep breath. "Look, there's really very little to connect us with him," she said. "Maybe somebody will remember us with him in the bar, but nobody knows that we came home with him, do they?"

Katherine just stared at her.

"So," Sandra continued, "if we can get rid of any trace of us here, then nobody would ever know we were here, would they?"

Katherine frowned. She was concentrating on what Sandra had just said.

"Katherine, please," Sandra begged. "Cooperate with me. I'm just trying to get us out of this mess in the best way possible. Now, all you have to do is tell me what you touched, and I'll take care of it. Can you do that?"

Katherine shook her head. "I don't know about this, Sandra. Don't they have ways of tracking people down?"

"If we don't leave any evidence, how can they find us?"

"But," Katherine protested, "what about the bar? That waitress saw us with him."

"I know, I know," Sandra sighed. "But who'd remember us? It's Friday night and she was very busy—and everybody else there was probably drunk. It's a chance we've just got to take—unless you want to call the police."

Katherine shuddered. "No!"

"Okay," Sandra said. "So all you have to do is tell me what you touched, and then you can go and sit in the other room and wait for me. But don't touch anything in there."

Katherine rubbed her hand across her forehead. "I can't remember."

"All right," Sandra said. "I'll just have to wipe off everything in this room that we might have touched." She went into the bathroom and got a towel. "Go and sit in the other room." She went to the door and opened it with the towel.

Katherine picked up her purse and went through the door.

The living room seemed so strangely calm after the horror of the bedroom. The stereo receiver was still on, but the record had shut off automatically. Katherine thought about turning the receiver off and then realized that it didn't matter. She sat down on the couch, wishing she could just put on her coat and run out of the apartment. She could hear the sound of running water in the bathroom.

In about ten minutes Sandra emerged from the bedroom. "I'm sure I got everything," she said. "Are you ready?"

Katherine leaped up. "Wait a minute," she said. "I want to check something." She brushed past her.

"You don't have to—" Sandra said. But Katherine was already in the other room.

Sandra got their coats. "Well?" she said when Katherine returned.

"I—I just wanted to double-check," Katherine said, putting on her coat.

Sandra glanced around the room. "Okay," she said. "Let's go."

The door clicked behind them, and they walked very carefully and quietly down the stairs. At the front door of the building they peered out into the street and waited for a single car to go by. Then they went out the door, down the steps, and walked rapidly away from the building. Sandra looked back briefly over her shoulder, and then turned her head and went on.

## CHAPTER FOUR

"Sandra, you've got to help me."

"You know I will. But what more do you want me to do?"

Katherine studied her hands, trying to find the right words. She was slouched on a chair in their living room, still in the same position she had collapsed in when they arrived home half an hour before. Sandra had perched herself gingerly on the couch on the opposite side of the room, favoring the side where the welts from Ted's beating still stung her. She was tired and she wanted to go to bed, but she knew that Katherine wanted to talk. She had done nothing but talk about the murder ever since they got home. Sandra was sure that Katherine was still in a state of shock.

Katherine looked up at her. "You're the only one I can trust now."

"Of course you can trust me," Sandra said quickly.

Katherine dropped her eyes. "Yes, but you're the only one in the world I can talk to because you're the only one who knows."

"Hey, we're in this thing together."

Katherine shook her head sadly. "It's not the

same for you. You're only in it because of me. *I'm* the one who actually—who actually killed him." The last words were barely a whisper.

Sandra did not agree, but she did not say so. The vision she had had, staring at the body, the blood, flashed through her mind. She pushed it away. "How do you want me to help you?" she asked.

"I—I don't know," Katherine stammered. "I guess I just want you to *be* here . . . to help me get through the next few days . . . or maybe the rest of my *life*." She was on the verge of tears.

"I'm not going anywhere."

Katherine looked up at her and smiled hopefully. She was glad that one of them was strong.

"Listen, I'm tired," Sandra said. "Let's go to bed."

Katherine sighed. "I don't think I can sleep."

"Take a pill."

"It won't work."

"Then take two," Sandra snapped. Then, more softly, "Don't worry, you'll be out like a light in five minutes. Really, it's the best thing. There's no point in our talking about it any more tonight."

Finally they went to bed. Sandra was exhausted. She longed to sleep, but the pain from the welts on her hip kept her awake. She got up and went into the bathroom to put some ointment on them, wincing as she rubbed the salve in. The pain brought the image of Ted Hanley to her mind: she could see his teeth and narrowed eyes again, could hear the whir of the belt as it came flying through the air, could feel the buckle biting into her flesh. Her fists clenched in outrage at the memory. She took a mirror and studied the angry welts already beginning to purple, and discovered that in some places the skin was broken. So, he had drawn blood. And had paid for her blood with his own—paid dearly.

She heard a sound coming from Katherine's bedroom and went to her door and slowly pushed it open. The light from the bathroom shone into the dark room and Sandra could see Katherine tossing restlessly in her sleep.

She walked soundlessly to the edge of Katherine's bed and gazed down on her. Katherine must be dreaming; her face was contorted and she was moaning. "No!" she suddenly said distinctly and then something that sounded like "Daddy."

So she wants her daddy, Sandra thought, torn between compassion and contempt. Did she think her rich and powerful father would save her from being punished for murder?

Sandra stood there, silently watching her for several more minutes and then went out, leaving the door open. She was not sleepy anymore. It was the first time she had been alone all day and she needed it to mull over what had happened. She went to the living room, turned on a light, and stretched out on the couch.

How she loved being alone in this apartment. When Katherine was away, or asleep, as now, it became almost her own, though nearly everything in it was Katherine's—and looked it. Cool and subdued and expensive.

The couch, covered in a nubby, oatmeal-colored fabric, a shade or two lighter than the area rug on the floor in front of it, was big and overstuffed.

Across the room were two chrome and canvas chairs, copies of a design Sandra had seen in the Museum of Modern Art. She had often thought how like Katherine those chairs were, sleek and handsome.

At the other end of the room were a dining table and chairs. The table had a smoked-glass top just like the coffee table in front of the couch. The apartment faced south, and Katherine had taken advantage of the light to nurture a profusion of plants.

The walls of the room were almost completely covered with artwork, and the neutral colors of the furnishings seemed to serve as a backdrop to the bright colors on the walls. Her own particular favorite was a large portrait of Katherine done by a college friend. At first glance it did not look that much like Katherine, but if you studied it, and if you knew Katherine, you could see the resemblance. She was sitting on the floor, one knee drawn up to her chest, looking pensively off to the side. Sandra had often seen Katherine sitting just that way, and the artist had captured her attitude perfectly.

The light was shining off Katherine's dark, glossy hair, and her deep-set gray eyes seemed to hint at secret thoughts Sandra would never know.

How she loved that portrait. It captivated her, and yet there were times she could barely look at it, so acutely did it remind her of the ordinariness of her own looks—looks that no one had ever wanted to recreate on canvas. The only modeling offers she had ever had were from men who were itching to get her clothes off. She had turned them down flat. If only she could look like Katherine . . .

Funny, that had been her very thought the first time she ever saw her. She had only been with the company a few days then and didn't know many people. Trying to make friends, she stopped to talk to Connie Maddox, a secretary who looked approachable. While she was standing there, Katherine walked by.

"Wow, I'd give anything to look like that," Sandra remarked to Connie after Katherine had gone. "Who *is* she?"

"You must mean Katherine Fielding?" Connie responded, making a face.

"What's wrong with her?" Sandra asked, interested.

"Oh, nothing really," Connie said. "She just thinks she's a little better than the rest of us, is all."

Sandra wasn't surprised. Anybody as beautiful as that had a right to be somewhat stand-offish.

A few days later Katherine came into the library. She walked past Sandra's desk without so much as a glance in her direction and strode purposefully toward the files. With envy, Sandra watched the long, graceful stretch of her legs, the patrician, almost regal, bearing of her head and shoulders. She longed to speak to Katherine, but couldn't summon the nerve.

After several minutes Katherine put back the file she had been looking at and turned to go. For the first time, she seemed to be aware of Sandra's presence and gave her a constrained smile as she walked toward the door.

Encouraged, Sandra said brightly, "Did you find

what you were looking for?" Then she added, "If you did, it's a miracle."

At the sound of Sandra's voice a flicker of curiosity appeared in Katherine's eyes. "Why do you say that?" she asked, stopping in front of Sandra's desk.

"Because," Sandra said, gesturing toward the files and stacks of books, "this place is a disaster. I've really got my work cut out for me."

Katherine looked skeptical. "You don't mean you're actually going to try and get this place organized, do you?"

Sandra nodded emphatically. "Just give me a couple of weeks."

Katherine studied her for a moment. "Well, if you do," she said, "you'll gain the undying gratitude of everyone in Editorial."

Sandra smiled at her. "Is that where you work?"

Katherine nodded. "I'm an assistant editor. It means I get to do all the dirty work." She started to edge away.

"What's your name, by the way?" Sandra said quickly. "Mine's Sandra."

Katherine flashed her a genuine smile. "Katherine," she said. "And welcome to the company, Sandra. We need people like you around here." Then she was gone.

Sandra was pleased with the way things had gone at that first meeting. She felt she had scored points with Katherine when she said she was going to get the library straightened up. Gaining Katherine's respect was important if she was going to become her friend. And that she was determined to do, because there was something about Katherine that had struck her, something that reminded her of someone special.

So whenever she saw Katherine she made a point of talking to her. Katherine even seemed flattered by the attention, so one day Sandra grew bold and asked her to lunch.

Sandra did most of the talking, but Katherine appeared interested in what she had to say. She asked Sandra a number of questions, especially about her background, and Sandra found herself rambling on.

She talked about her marriage to Erik Jurgenson and their subsequent divorce, playing up the aspects that she thought a feminist like Katherine would like to hear: how Erik tried to make her quit her teaching job and have children; how he constantly expected her to defer to his wishes; how he only wanted her to be an extension of his identity, instead of a person in her own right.

Of course, she did not mention her own faults in the dissolution of the marriage: how she had married Erik solely for convenience, though she had led him to believe that she loved him (men were so easily fooled); how she had been happy enough at first. But how quickly the novelty had worn off! It was then that she had begun to flirt outrageously with Erik's friends, more to break the monotony of married life than because she felt any real attraction. She had goaded Erik into the divorce, not because he had been to blame but because she was bored with him, with marriage, with the Midwest.

And, too, she did not go into the kind of life she had been living since she came to New York: the depressing, menial jobs she had taken in the beginning; the endless array of men she had gone to bed with; and the searing loneliness that frantic sex could not cure. She did not think someone like Katherine would like to hear about that. Or would even understand it.

Katherine remarked that she had once spent a summer in the Midwest. In fact, her mother's family was from there, and she was curious to know what growing up in the Midwest had been like for Sandra. So Sandra had described for her what it was like living in a bland, middle-class environment, and especially what it was like being the only daughter in a family with two younger brothers and being female in what seemed to her to be a very male-oriented world. When Katherine asked about her mother, Sandra had tried to explain to her that her mother had always seemed like a creature apart. And then she had suddenly realized just who Katherine reminded her of—it was her mother. They were both beautiful, cool, aloof and serenely self-assured—figures to aspire to, not to love; objects to adore, and to hate. But Sandra had not told Katherine that she reminded her of her mother, not then or since.

That lunch was the beginning of their friendship. Still, it had mostly been Sandra's doing. It had been like a courtship on her part, but she had eventually won Katherine over. Up to a point. There was a part of Katherine that was still remote—and private. Even after they had become

good, close friends, Katherine had never invited
Sandra to her apartment—though she had visited
Sandra's tiny, cramped quarters on the West Side
several times.

When Sandra did finally manage to see Katherine's apartment it was more a result of an unhappy accident than by any design.

Erik was in town on business trip and asked
her out to dinner—"for old times' sake." Against
her better judgment, Sandra accepted. They had
begun with drinks, and with each drink he took,
Erik had grown increasingly abusive. Feeling
guilty, Sandra endured his barbs and taunts, picking at her dinner in silent misery. She had wanted
nothing so much as to go home, but Erik had
insisted on going to a discotheque. Reluctantly, to
appease him, Sandra had taken him to a crowded,
noisy place on Eighty-sixth Street, but once on
the dance floor he began raving at her, outshouting
the music with a stream of abuse. Gradually, other dancers began to shy away from them. They
had begun to draw stares and then muttered comments, and Sandra, feeling utterly humiliated,
had fled. Fighting back the tears, she raced into
the street and began looking around for a cab,
until a sudden thought flashed into her mind:
Katherine lived nearby. On an impulse, she went
to Katherine's building and had the doorman an-
nounce her.

When Katherine opened the door she seemed
surprised and slightly annoyed—until she saw
Sandra's face.

"Look, Katherine, I'm sorry to bother you like

this," Sandra blurted out before Katherine could say anything, "but I'm kind of upset, and I just want to talk to you."

As soon as she walked inside, the tears came. Without a word, Katherine put her arm around Sandra and led her to the couch. She disappeared for a moment and came back with a handful of tissues. "Here," she said, giving them to Sandra, "let it all out." She sat down next to her and let her cry for a while before she said softly, "It was Erik, wasn't it? You told me today you were going to see him."

Sandra wiped at her eyes. "Yes, I saw him," she sniffled, "and it was the stupidest thing I've ever done."

"What did he do to you?" Katherine asked.

"I guess he had too much to drink, because he started saying terrible things to me," Sandra sobbed. "He—he called me names—horrible, vile names—and told me what a worthless bitch I was and how he was glad to be rid of me." She started crying again. "He made a scene. Oh, Katherine, it was awful, just awful." She lapsed into loud sobs.

After a minute, Katherine said, "But don't you see what he was doing, Sandra? He was trying to get back at you because you hurt him. He didn't say those things because he was drunk, he's probably been planning something like this ever since you divorced him and left Minneapolis."

Sandra stared at her through the tears. "Do you really think so?"

Katherine nodded. "Of course. It was obviously spite, pure and simple. Naturally, it hurt, but you can't let the things he said get to you."

"But they were so *awful*."

"That's the way he intended them to be. But you've got to forget about him now—that part of your life is over."

"Oh, I know, I know," Sandra said, wringing her hands. "I must have been a fool to see him in the first place."

Katherine grabbed her hand. "Stop thinking like that," she said. "How were you to know what he'd do?"

Frightened by the intensity of feeling she had at Katherine's touch, Sandra pulled away from her and started to get up. "Thanks for listening to me," she said. "I'm fine now, and I think I'd better go. I know I'm imposing on you."

"Don't be silly," Katherine said, pushing her back down on the couch. "You're not going anywhere until you're a lot calmer. How about a glass of brandy? Think that would help?"

"Sure. Sounds wonderful."

"Okay," Katherine said. "I'll get you one." She stood up. "Now, take off your coat and make yourself comfortable."

While Katherine went for the brandy Sandra got out of her coat and took her first good look at Katherine's apartment. It was just as she imagined it would be, elegant and somewhat understated—much like Katherine herself. She thought fleetingly of her own apartment and wished that she had a place like this instead.

When Katherine came back with the brandy in wafer-thin snifters, they sat and talked some more until Sandra was feeling almost mellow, and Katherine herself was yawning. Finally, Katherine said, "Look I'm really tired and I've got to get to bed, but I don't think you should go home by yourself. Why don't you spend the night here? You can sleep on the couch."

Sandra tried to protest, but Katherine persisted and Sandra ended up spending the night. In the morning she woke early and lay on the couch a long time, just gazing at the things in the living room. Katherine's portrait particularly caught her eye.

After a while she got up and got dressed. While she was waiting for Katherine, she walked around the apartment. It was really just a one-bedroom, but there was an alcove off the living room that an earlier tenant had enclosed—probably for a child's room—and Katherine was using it for an office. When Sandra saw that room it gave her an idea.

Over the next few weeks she put her plan into action, complaining repeatedly to Katherine about how unhappy she was with her dingy, furnished room and how she would like to move to something better but couldn't afford it. Katherine had been sympathetic and even admitted that she herself was paying too much rent but that in the long run it was worth it to have a decent apartment. Then, carefully, Sandra had broached the subject of the extra room. Couldn't she move in there and share Katherine's rent? It would certainly be a solution for both of them.

Katherine had been cool to the idea at first, so Sandra had not pushed it. But one day she mentioned that her lease was coming up for renewal and that she would have to pay an increase in rent, and Sandra had seized upon that. After a few days Katherine relented, and Sandra moved in the next week.

And now their friendship had brought them to this night, to murder. How improbable it all seemed that she, little Sandy Lund from Mound, Minnesota, should find herself mixed up in murder. And yet . . . it was the most exciting thing that had ever happened to her.

She had never seen so much blood before. It was really amazing how much there had been. Sandra lay on the couch, replaying the murder in her mind, watching brass and leather gleam ominously in the air, poised to strike like some vicious snake; seeing again the malevolent smile turn to terror as the weapon found its mark, the blood . . . oh, God, the blood. Finally, fatigue overtook her excitement and she fell asleep under the peaceful gaze of Katherine's portrait.

She woke to find Katherine staring down at her, a drink in her hand, a half-empty bottle of Chivas Regal on the table beside her.

"Hey, aren't you hitting the booze kind of hard?" Sandra asked, sitting up.

Katherine ignored the question. She plopped herself in a chair, one leg bent under her and the other drawn up to her chin. She tucked the edges of her bathrobe around her feet.

"Katherine, what do you think you're doing?" Sandra asked, a little more insistent this time.

"I'm trying to stay unconscious," Katherine muttered.

"Okay, go right ahead," Sandra said, annoyed. Did Katherine think she was the only one involved? What about *her* feelings? But no, Katherine wasn't interested at all in what Sandra might be going through. "Okay," she said. "Feel sorry for yourself. It's not going to help."

Katherine slammed her drink down on the table. "Is that what I'm doing?" she cried. "Feeling sorry for myself? My God, Sandra, have you forgotten what happened last night?"

"Don't be ridiculous. Of course I haven't forgotten. We've got to check to see if he's been found yet."

"Don't bother. I already listened to the news on the radio."

"And?"

"Nothing—so far."

"Well, obviously his roommate hasn't come back yet—and nobody else seems to have missed him."

"Maybe it's a trap. Maybe the police are trying to lull us into complacency."

"That's absurd. He just hasn't been found yet." Something in Katherine's manner roused her to anger. Before she could stop herself she heard a harshness creep into her voice. "And when he is," she went on cruelly, "I'm sure there'll be a big, juicy story on it. I mean it's got all the elements: a nude body; plush East Side apartment; big, important advertising agency—"

"Stop it!" Katherine shouted.

Sandra looked at her. "Hey, listen, you'd better get used to it, Katherine. And you'd better start preparing yourself for it if we're going to pull this off."

"What do you mean 'prepare myself'?"

Sandra leaned forward in her chair. "Come Monday, Katherine," she said very deliberately, as if she were talking to a child, "you're going to have to give the best performance of your life. You'll have to act as if nothing has happened."

"I—I don't think I can do it."

"You don't have any choice."

Katherine drained her drink, and sat swirling the ice in her glass, sipping the water as it melted. Then she looked up. "Sandra," she said hesitantly, there's something I think you'd better know about."

Sandra's brow furrowed. "What is it?"

"It—it's in my purse." Katherine looked around her. "Must be in my room," she said and started to get up.

"Sit down," Sandra said. "I'll get it." She went into Katherine's room and came back out, carrying the purse. She handed it to Katherine.

"No," Katherine said, pushing it away. "You look."

Puzzled, Sandra opened the bag and looked inside. "I don't see anything," she said.

"In the bottom," Katherine said softly.

Sandra reached into the bag. She fished around for several seconds and then brought her hand out. In it was the letter opener.

"So that's what you went back for," Sandra said under her breath. She stared wide-eyed at the long, slender blade and the ornate handle with its initialed "H." Without moving her head she shifted her eyes to look at Katherine. "Why?" she said. It was not a question, but an accusation.

Katherine lowered her eyes. "I don't know," she

said. "When we were getting ready to go, I just had the feeling that I was leaving something behind. So I went back in there and—"

"But I washed it off and put it on the desk," Sandra interjected. "That's where it came from, didn't it?"

Katherine nodded. "I saw it there and—I took it." She rubbed her hand across her forehead. "I don't know why, I just didn't want to leave it."

Sandra sighed and sat down. "Well, you've done it," she said. "Now I'll have to get rid of it."

"How?"

"I don't know how. It's not something you can just drop in the garbage, that's for sure."

"We could throw it in the river."

"Oh, sure, and risk somebody seeing us do it. That's really a brilliant idea, Katherine."

Katherine bit her lip. "I guess I botched it all up, didn't I?"

Sandra shook her head. "Don't worry about it. It's not that important." Suddenly a wary look came over her face. "Unless you touched the desk when you picked it up. You didn't do that, did you?"

"Oh, no," Katherine said. "I was careful about that."

"Well, that's good. As for this"—Sandra considered the letter opener in her hand—"I guess I can figure out a way to get rid of it. So, don't get upset about it. But please—just don't pull any more surprises on me." She lifted her eyes to Katherine's. "There aren't any more, are there?"

"No," Katherine said quickly and looked away. She took a deep breath. "Well . . . yes. Maybe it won't matter to you, but it does to me. It's why—why I think I went after him with the letter opener."

"Because you had to. It was the only way of stopping him."

"Maybe. But there's more to it than that," Katherine said slowly. "You see—I kind of freaked out."

"Well, so did I," Sandra said emphatically. She rubbed her sore hip. "When he started hitting me with that belt, I could have killed him myself."

"That's what I'm talking about. The moment I saw that belt and he—he hit you with it, I just didn't know what I was doing. It was so—" Katherine's voice broke. "It was so familiar to me."

Sandra looked mystified. "Familiar? How could it be familiar?"

Katherine turned her face away and stared out the window. "It's hard to talk about even now," she said. Finally, she turned back to face Sandra. "My father used to beat me up with a belt just like that when I was a little girl." Her voice had trailed off into a whisper, but her eyes bored into Sandra's.

Sandra stared back at her. "So that's why you hate him," she said softly.

"Yeah, that's why. I never understood it—but I never forgot it."

"No, how could you? Did he—did it happen often?"

Katherine nodded her head. "Yes. More than I care to remember. I was only eleven the first time it happened, and the last time was when I was sixteen—just before I went away to Smith."

"What about your mother?"

"She never knew. I never told her."

"Why not?"

"Because you just didn't talk about things like that in our family. But I suppose she must have known. My brother knew, I think. He started treating me a little nicer, I guess he felt sorry for me. But he was still afraid of my father, even though he was older than I was."

"So you never told *anyone*?"

"Well, I saw a psychiatrist for a while, and I told her. That was hard to do, too. Even though it was ten years later I still felt ashamed."

"*Ashamed*?"

"Yes. I thought it was all my fault, that I had brought it on myself. Even though I never did anything, really, to deserve it."

"What did your shrink say?"

"Oh, she said she thought it was a sexual thing on my father's part. That only made it worse. That's when I stopped going to see her."

Sandra said nothing. She seemed to be thinking about what she had just learned, putting it all in place.

Katherine sighed heavily. "So, when I saw that belt last night, I guess I went a little crazy."

"Sure," Sandra said. "I'm no psychiatrist, but it's not hard to figure out what happened."

Sandra stared thoughtfully at Katherine. She had never seen such a look of appeal on Katherine's face before. No, Katherine had always seemed so sure of herself. And now here she was, almost begging Sandra to understand, to say it was all right. Suddenly she realized just how much Katherine had come to depend on her.

\* \* \*

Frank MacLaughlin and Harry Gross were the two detectives who responded to the call. By the time they arrived on East Seventy-seventh Street from the Nineteenth Precinct on East Sixty-seventh, two patrolmen were already there, dispatched by radio. One of the patrolmen showed the detectives into the bedroom where the body was.

"Who's the guy in the living room?" MacLaughlin asked him.

"Roommate."

"He do this?" Gross asked, indicating the body.

"I dunno," the patrolman said. "He *says* he just got home, and this guy looks like he's been dead a couple of days." He wrinkled his nose. "Smells like it, too."

"Okay," MacLaughlin said. "I'll get his statement in a minute. Go back in there with him."

The two detectives made a cursory survey of the body and the room and then exchanged a look that meant they were both thinking the same thing: a homosexual slaying.

Then MacLaughlin saw the photos of the nude women on the wall and pointed them out to his partner. Gross looked at them and shrugged.

Both detectives began taking notes. They took in the condition and position of the body on the bed, the belt lying on the floor, some clothes strewn on a chair—a grotesque scene, made the more bizarre by the uncanny neatness of the rest of the room. MacLaughlin glanced into the adjoining bathroom. It looked undisturbed.

"Okay, I'm going to talk to the roommate," Mac-Laughlin said. "You call in."

Barry Goldman was seated on the couch, his head in his hands, when MacLaughlin strode into the living room and sat down next to him. He looked up at him nervously.

"I'm Detective MacLaughlin. Could you give me your name, please?" MacLaughlin said, his pencil ready.

Goldman sighed. "Barry Goldman."

"Date of birth?"

"April 12, 1941."

"This your apartment?"

"Yes."

"What's the victim's name?"

Goldman turned pale. "I—I'm not sure."

"What do you mean, you're not sure?" Mac-Laughlin asked, perplexed. "I thought he was your roommate?"

Goldman was shaking. "I *suppose* it's my roommate," he said reluctantly. "But I can't say for sure. Because—because I didn't really look at him."

"Would you mind looking now?"

Goldman swallowed. "Do I have to?" he said weakly.

"I'm afraid so. We want you to identify him, if you can." MacLaughlin stood up.

Goldman inhaled deeply and got unsteadily to his feet. He followed the detective into the bedroom.

MacLaughlin went around to the side of the bed and motioned to Goldman to stand next to him. Then he leaned over and carefully lifted

Ted Hanley's head so that Goldman could see his face. The features were distorted and the eyes were open, staring straight ahead, unseeing.

Goldman gaped at the face for a second and then shut his eyes. He turned to walk away, but he was swaying, and MacLaughlin grabbed his arm.

"Let's go back in the living room," MacLaughlin said, steering him to the couch. "Can I have a drink?" Goldman asked dully.

"Sure," MacLaughlin said. "Where is it?"

Goldman pointed to the kitchen.

MacLaughlin went into the kitchen and came back holding a glass with some brandy in it. He put it in Goldman's hand.

Goldman took several swallows and then leaned back. "Okay," he said. "Let's get this over with."

MacLaughlin took out his notebook again. "I take it that's your roommate," he said matter-of-factly.

Goldman blinked. "Yeah. That's Ted."

"What's his full name?"

"Edward Hanley. I think his middle name's Victor."

"He lived here?"

"Yes."

"Date of birth?"

"I'm not exactly sure. I know we're . . . uh, he was . . . the same age."

"How long did you know the victim?"

"I guess about fifteen or sixteen years. We went to college together. Cornell."

"How long did you live with the victim?"

Goldman stared at him angrily. "Look, do you

have to keep calling him 'the victim'? He was my friend and now he's . . ."

MacLaughlin studied him. "Okay," he said. "How long did you live with Mr. Hanley?"

"Eight or nine months. I moved in with him after my divorce. I'm on the road a lot and it didn't make any sense to spend a lot of money on a place of my own—especially after the divorce settlement. And then Ted seemed eager to have me move in. He's always been kind of crazy with money, and I think he wanted someone to share expenses."

MacLaughlin looked around the room. "Did he have many debts?"

"Sure. Oh, you mean gambling debts, things like that?"

MacLaughlin nodded.

"No, he just had expensive tastes. I guess he lived beyond his means."

"When was the last time you saw the—Mr. Hanley—alive?"

Goldman thought for a moment. "I suppose it must have been last Thursday night. I just saw him for a little while when I came in. I told him I was going away for the weekend. But I heard him getting up the next day as I was leaving for work. I didn't see him, though, and I didn't come back that night." He shook his head sadly, and fell silent.

MacLaughlin watched the emotions play across Goldman's face, then continued the questioning, taking a softer tack. Goldman seemed to have relaxed somewhat and the answers came more readily.

Yes, he was sure that Ted had gone to work on Friday. That was the one thing Ted was really reliable about. He was an account executive with an ad agency and he seemed to like his job—although he complained about it a lot.

No, he had noticed nothing unusual when he came in tonight—except for the smell. And the fact that the front door had not been double-locked. His roommate was fanatic about that. He always bolted himself in. Also, the lights and the stereo receiver were on, so that at first he had thought Ted was home and had someone in his room.

Yes, Ted did that often. There were a lot of women. No, he didn't really know any of them since Ted usually picked them up in bars. He *had* known a couple of Ted's previous girlfriends, but he was sure that Ted hadn't seen either of them in a long time. Yes, he thought he could give the police their names and telephone numbers.

Yes, Ted was strictly heterosexual. What kind of question was that? But—maybe he shouldn't say this—he did think Ted might have liked doing some kinky things with women. Like what? Well, he couldn't be sure, but he thought that Ted liked beating them up—just a little. No, he had no proof of that, but Ted had kind of hinted about it. And one morning he had come in just as Ted was leaving with a girl. She had tried to hide her face, but he had seen a big bruise on it. Later, he had asked Ted about that, and Ted had just looked at him and laughed. And another thing: Ted seemed to like making it with two women. That he was sure of, because he had bragged about it. No, he couldn't say who any of these women were. He rarely saw them and when he did they were never the same ones.

No, he didn't really know which bars Ted liked to hang out in. He didn't much care for that scene himself. But he was pretty sure that Ted only liked to go to bars on the East Side. "The only place to find Grade-A Prime," he always said.

No, he didn't really know Ted's family. He thought they lived somewhere in New Jersey. But Ted never talked about them and only went to see them infrequently.

Of course, he would supply the police with the names of other friends of Ted's who might be helpful.

No, he had no idea who could have murdered Ted—or why. And as far as he could tell, nothing seemed to be missing from the apartment—except that he hadn't really looked around Ted's room. Anyway, he wasn't sure if he could tell because he didn't go in there very often.

"Would you mind checking the room now?"

Goldman shuddered. "I don't want to look at him again."

"You don't have to. Just look around the room and tell me if anything strikes you or if anything seems to be missing."

Gritting his teeth and averting his eyes from the body, Goldman did what MacLaughlin ordered. He peered into the dresser and desk drawers as MacLaughlin opened them with his handkerchief, and then they looked through the closet.

"Well?" MacLaughlin asked.

"I don't think there's anything missing," Goldman responded. Then he walked over to the desk.

He hesitated. "I think Ted had a silver letter opener," he said. "I didn't see it in the drawers. But I
think he kept it on top of the desk, here. It was a
family heirloom and it had a fancy handle with a
big 'H' on it."

MacLaughlin raised an eyebrow. The murder
weapon?

"What about that belt on the floor next to the
body? Ever seen it before?" MacLaughlin asked.

Goldman stared at the belt. "I don't know," he
said uncertainly. "It may be Ted's."

"Okay. Thanks," MacLaughlin said. "You can
go back in the other room now. But you'll have to
come down to the station house to make a statement."

Goldman nodded and walked out of the room.

Other policemen had been filtering into the
apartment while MacLaughlin had been talking
to Goldman, and they were busy going about their
various routines. One of the crime lab men came
up to MacLaughlin and reported that he had
found something odd: there were no fingerprints
anywhere in the bedroom or adjoining bathroom,
not even a smudged or latent one. Even if the
room had been recently cleaned, there still should
have been smudged prints on the doorknobs. That
could only mean one thing: the killer had wiped
off the prints.

From what Goldman had told him, Frank Mac-
Laughlin had already begun theorizing about the
murder. It could have been done by a woman (or
women) who had been frightened by Mr. Hanley's
S&M tendencies and had fought back. But the
fingerprints being wiped away. . . . Did it mean

the murder was premeditated? Revenge? Could be. In the meantime, there was not much to go on. They had to start somewhere, though. And it seemed to MacLaughlin the best place to find the answer would be in the victim's own environment. That meant the East Side bars.

## CHAPTER FIVE

Sandra was up and nearly dressed before she realized that she had not heard a sound from Katherine's room. So she went to her door, knocked sharply on it, and then pushed it open.

Katherine was still in bed, but not asleep.

"Get up," Sandra ordered.

Katherine groaned and turned away from her. "I can't."

"Oh, no you don't. You're going to work if I have to drag you there."

Katherine sat up. "I just can't face it."

Sandra walked to the bed and looked down fiercely at her. "I don't care. You're not going to fink out now." Then her tone softened. "Besides, the longer you put it off the harder it'll get."

Katherine's chest heaved. "But what am I going to say to people?"

"Nothing. Absolutely nothing. If anybody asks what you did over the weekend just say you hung around with me and it was a quiet one. Nobody cares, anyway."

"I care."

"I know. Just don't let it show. Now, come on,

get dressed. We should check the papers and I want to make sure we have plenty of time."

Katherine threw off the bed covers and sat on the edge of the bed. "You think he's been found yet?"

"I wouldn't be at all surprised. If he hasn't, he will be soon. Please, Katherine! Get a move on, will you?"

At the newsstand on the corner of Eighty-sixth Street, Sandra bought both the *Times* and the *Daily News*. She glanced idly at the front pages of both newspapers as they stood waiting for the crosstown bus. When Katherine queried her with her eyes, Sandra shook her head almost imperceptibly.

The bus was not too crowded and they went straight to the back and sat down. Sandra casually opened the *News*. It was there on the second page: "Ad Exec Slain in Posh E. Side Pad." She skimmed the story: ". . . discovered by his roommate Sunday night . . . no weapon was found on the scene . . . no motive has been established . . . police are checking . . ."

"It's okay," Sandra said quietly to Katherine. "Do you want to read it?"

Katherine shook her head. "Not now."

There was also a small item in the *Times*. It did not give any more information than was in the *News*.

Sandra smiled to herself. They had gotten away with it. Their link to Ted was so tenuous she was sure the police would never discover it. So they were safe. All she had to worry about now was

Katherine. She glanced sideways at her. She seemed okay, staring idly at the people boarding the bus. As if she felt Sandra's gaze, she suddenly turned and whispered, "Is it really okay, or did you just say that?"

"Of course it's okay," Sandra shot back. This time it was she who looked away. They made the rest of the trip in silence. It was not till they were entering the Roth Building that Sandra dared another sidelong glance. Katherine looked too pale.

"When you get to your office," Sandra said to her, "put some blusher on."

"Why? What's wrong?" Katherine said, feeling her face.

"You look like death warmed over."

"You have such an apt way of putting things, Sandra," Katherine said sarcastically.

"Well, you don't want anybody to notice, do you?"

"Of course not."

"Then do it. And try to remember to be your usual jovial self—especially with Vivian." She was referring to the young black woman who shared Katherine's office.

"Vivian?" Katherine's ashen face grew even paler. "Oh, God, that's going to be hard. She's going to take one look at me and know something's wrong. She always does."

"Then tell her you're still pissed off about the promotion."

"What if she doesn't believe me?"

"Why shouldn't she? Just be cool, that's all."

They had made their way to the elevators now and Sandra spied a man from the company. "Good morning," she said cheerily, directing a smile at him. Katherine merely nodded.

"Hi, Sandra, Katherine," he answered. "How was your weekend?"

"Oh, just great," Sandra said. Then, quickly, "How was yours?"

"Let me tell you," he said as they stepped into the elevator. "I did the stupidest thing." And he started giving Sandra all the details of his weekend project. When they reached the reception area he was still talking, and Sandra was smiling and nodding at him. But over his shoulder she watched Katherine glance back at her and then walk stiffly away.

Vivian was already at her desk.

"Hiya, Katie," Vivian said. She was the only person who ever called Katherine by a nickname.

"Morning, Viv," Katherine responded.

"How're ya doin'? How was the weekend?"

Katherine stared at her, suddenly overwhelmed by a perverse desire to say, "Fine, Viv. Just fine. I killed a man over the weekend. What do you think of that?" But she said nothing.

Vivian gave her a searching look. Then she suddenly slapped her hand to her mouth. "Oh, shit," she said. "I'm sorry. I forgot. I heard about the job."

Katherine sat down at her desk. "Oh. Who told you?" She had to get Vivian talking about the promotion, had to pretend she still cared.

"Uh," Vivian stammered, "Bruce told us all right away." She looked wryly at Katherine, "And I figured they weren't handing out *two* promotions."

"He sure didn't waste any time, did he?"

"Hell no. He was so happy he was probably drunk the whole weekend."

"Good. Maybe he'll get cirrhosis and Charles'll have to give the job to me."

Vivian laughed. "I'm glad to see you haven't lost your sense of humor."

Katherine smiled sardonically. But she was pleased with herself. She had pulled it off. Vivian didn't suspect. Maybe, just maybe, it was going to be all right.

She had been at work about an hour when Stan Herzberg appeared at the door.

Katherine looked up and scowled.

Stan ignored her look. He smiled at her. "I'd like to talk to you," he said.

"Okay." She pointed to the chair next to her desk. "Sit down."

Vivian was on the phone. She looked at Stan's back and raised her eyebrows to Katherine.

"Well?" Katherine asked Stan.

"I'd like to clear up that little misunderstanding we had on Friday," he said. "I was rude to you. I'm sorry."

Katherine was taken aback. The last thing she had expected was an apology from Stan Herzberg. She looked at him blankly.

Stan lowered his voice. "You don't have to explain. I realize now that you were upset. But I didn't know. I think it's a real shame."

"I don't understand," she said. She wondered what he was after, then quickly reproached herself. Maybe she had misjudged him.

"What Charles did to you," Stan was explaining. "I heard later. You deserved that job, but, well, there's just no accounting for Charles sometimes."

Katherine stared at him. So she *had* been wrong. He was on her side. "Thanks for saying so." Her smile was grateful.

Stan smiled back at her. "Well, I try to keep track of the good people around here. And you're one of the best."

Katherine was touched. There was genuine warmth in his words.

"And as far as Friday is concerned," he went on, "it was just a little kidding between friends." He looked meaningfully at her.

"Oh, that," she said, waving the comment away. "I forgot all about it."

"Well, I'm glad we got that straightened out." He stood up. "Remember, if you ever have any problems here, you can come to me with them. Maybe we'll have lunch sometime, okay?"

Katherine nodded. "Yes, I'd like that."

"Good. Well, I won't keep you from your work any longer."

Katherine stared after him as he turned and left the office.

"What's he doin', Katie," Vivian said, hanging up the phone, "tryin' to put the make on you?"

"I'll be damned if I know." Katherine shook her head. "No, that's not fair. He was just being nice."

"I thought it was Sandra he had the hots for."

"So did I."

"Maybe she gave him the cold shoulder."

"Sandra? That'll be the day." Katherine laughed.

"I don't think she knows how to say no to a man. She says she doesn't like Stan, but she leads him on anyway."

"She'd better watch it. He's not the kind of guy to play games with."

"Oh, hell, Sandra can take care of herself." And she added to herself, ironically, just about everything else, too. Including me. She hoped Vivian hadn't caught the involuntary shudder that had run through her at the thought.

Sandra was putting a pile of books back on a shelf when she heard someone approaching. She did not turn around to see who it was. Suddenly a pair of strong hands gripped her around the waist. She knew immediately that it was Stan, but she was startled by the thrill that ran through her body.

"Hi, Stan," she said without looking. "You'd better stop. Someone might come in."

He released his hands and she turned to face him.

"I just talked to your friend Katherine," he said.

"What about?"

"That little run-in we had on Friday, remember?"

"Sure I remember. I'm surprised you talked to her about *that*."

"Well, I heard about what that crazy Charles did to her, and I wanted her to know I understand where she was coming from."

"Yeah, she was really upset about that promotion. Still is."

"I felt kind of sorry for her. She's really a nice kid, and that was a rotten thing for him to do. So I wanted her to know I'm on her side."

"That was very sweet of you, Stan."

"You know me, I'm just a nice guy." He grinned at her.

"The nicest," Sandra said, brushing her body against him as she walked over to her desk and sat down.

Stan followed her hungrily with his eyes. He was about to take a step toward her when suddenly there were voices in the corridor outside, and he hastily resumed his businesslike expression.

"I'd better get back to my office," he said reluctantly. "My girl must be wondering where I am. I've been gone a long time."

Sandra gave him a little pout. "You're so conscientious," she said. "But I have work to do, too. See you later."

He looked back over his shoulder and winked.

After Stan had gone, Sandra sat musing about her own strange reaction to him. She had never been aroused by Stan before, yet she found herself wondering what it would be like to go to bed with him. He was probably a lousy lover, but maybe not. Anyway, she never intended to find out.

Except . . . she could see the two of them in bed together: Stan on top of her, her hands on his back, her fingernails raking his skin. At first he would love it, but then she would sink them deeper and deeper, until she drew blood. Then he would squirm and try to get away, but she would hold him harder and thrust her nails deeper into his flesh until the blood would start to pour out of it. . . .

She shook herself. She was getting Stan mixed up with Ted Hanley. That was it. How funny the mind was, getting things and people all confused like that.

The bus was packed and they pushed to the back, where there was a little more space. Sandra balanced herself against a pole and opened the *Post*. There was another story about Ted, and Sandra began reading it. Katherine was looking over her shoulder.

Suddenly Katherine moaned and fell against her. Thrown off balance, Sandra staggered into a man standing next to her. "Sorry," she mumbled to the man as she grabbed for an overhead strap. Katherine was still leaning against her and Sandra twisted her neck to look at her. Her eyes were shut and her mouth was open as if she were gasping for air.

"What's wrong with you?" Sandra hissed. People were beginning to stare. It was making Sandra very uncomfortable.

Katherine's mouth was close to Sandra's ear. She whispered something incoherent, and all that Sandra could catch was what sounded like "eyes."

"What are you—" Sandra started to say. But then she suddenly realized what Katherine meant. There had been a picture of Ted Hanley in the paper. A portrait shot, in which he was looking straight into the camera, not smiling. "Oh, Christ," Sandra muttered to herself. She could feel Katherine's body trembling. She was afraid she was going to burst into tears any second.

Sandra moved quickly. She could not hazard a scene on the bus. She had to get Katherine out of there. Putting her arm around her for support, she began to propel her toward the door. Everyone around them was gawking. An elderly gentleman offered his assistance.

Katherine was confused. "Where are we going?" she said. "This isn't our stop."

"We're going to get a cab," Sandra said loudly for the benefit of the other passengers. "You're still too weak from the flu, and I'm afraid you're going to faint."

Before Katherine could protest, Sandra had maneuvered her to the exit and was half pushing, half carrying her off the bus. She had barely regained her balance when the bus pulled away in a cloud of fumes, leaving her, bewildered, on the sidewalk with Sandra's arm still around her.

"Are you okay?" Sandra asked.

Katherine nodded limply. "I'm really sorry, Sandra. I just couldn't help it. I saw his eyes, and I—"

"I understand," Sandra broke in. "Don't talk about it now," she said, looking frantically for a cab. "Wait till we get home."

By the time they finally got a cab and got upstairs to their apartment, Katherine had calmed down. Sandra tried to get her to talk, but she refused. Instead, she took two sleeping pills and retreated into her own room, shutting the door.

Okay, Sandra thought to herself, let her sleep

it off. It's probably the best thing for her—for now.

The six o'clock news had already started. Half-way through the program there was a brief report on Ted Hanley's murder. As the camera panned the outside of his building Sandra realized she would never have recognized it in the daytime. Then a reporter was interviewing a good-looking young detective with a determined expression. Sandra leaned closer to the set, concentrating, hearing him say there was no apparent motive and that the police were checking out all the leads.

*That means they don't have any leads.* Relief surged through her. *And they never will. Eventually they'll just give up and file it away as unsolved.* She felt very sure of herself.

She didn't have to worry about the police anymore. But Katherine, that was a different story. Sandra was very worried about Katherine. She tried to push it from her mind, but Katherine's near collapse on the bus, her helpless, dazed look haunted her while she busied herself making dinner, kept floating up at her from the TV. She forced herself to watch until the eleven o'clock news came on. They only gave the murder a passing mention, and this time there was no film. So she turned the set off and went to bed.

Just as she was drifting off to sleep she heard a muffled scream. It jerked her into consciousness. She raced to Katherine's door, threw it open and turned on the light.

Katherine was sitting up in bed, hugging herself.

"Did you scream?" Sandra asked anxiously.

Katherine didn't answer.

Sandra sat down on the edge of the bed. "Were you screaming?"

Still no answer. Katherine did not seem to be aware of Sandra's presence, so Sandra touched her arm. Katherine flinched. "Oh. It's you," she said.

"Who else would it be?"

"I don't know," Katherine said dully. "I was dreaming I guess."

"About him?"

Katherine looked startled. "Who?"

"You know. Ted."

Katherine stared at her for a moment and then looked quickly away. "Yes. This time."

"What do you mean 'this time'?"

There was a second of hesitation and then Katherine said, "I don't want to talk about it."

"You'll feel better if you do."

Katherine turned to look at her directly. Her eyes were filled with an infinite sadness. "No, Sandra," she said. "Your therapy numbers can't help me now. Just go back to bed."

Sandra opened her mouth to speak again, but something in Katherine's manner changed her mind. She got up and went to the door. "If you need me, don't be afraid to wake me up," she said quietly, and shut the door behind her.

Katherine reached over and turned off the light. She lay in the dark a long time, brooding about her nightmare, the nightmare that had been with her for so long and now had come true. So horribly true. Toward dawn she fell asleep.

*    *    *

The investigation into Ted Hanley's murder was going slowly. MacLaughlin was beginning to give up hope.

On Tuesday afternoon the results of the medical examiner's report came in: Ted Hanley had been dead between forty-eight and thirty-six hours before he was found. He had died immediately as the result of a single puncture wound to the heart which had severed the aorta, causing heavy blood loss. The instrument that had delivered the fatal wound had a relatively thick blade and it had been twisted in the wound—probably when it was being pulled out.

MacLaughlin had been pleased by the description of the blade. It tended to pinpoint as the murder weapon the letter opener the roommate had said was missing, and support his own theory that the murder was probably not premeditated. The killer had simply picked up the nearest weapon at hand. Still, whoever had done it had either known a lot about anatomy to hit the heart like that, with one blow—or it had been pure accident. And the severed aorta meant that the blood must have spurted out like crazy, so that the murderer's clothes would have been covered with it—unless he or she were naked, too.

But why had the killer taken the weapon away? After having gone to all the trouble of wiping off all other fingerprints, the killer could have easily wiped off the letter opener, too. Crazy. MacLaughlin shook his head. Experience had taught him that killers sometimes did crazy things: often they formed attachments to their weapons—and it was often their downfall.

By Thursday night he was less optimistic. The detectives had worked their way through the few leads they had, questioning all of Hanley's fellow tenants and co-workers. The tenants recognized Hanley's photo, which the roommate had secured for the police, but none of them had seen him over the weekend. From Hanley's co-workers they learned that he had definitely been to work on Friday and that they had noticed nothing peculiar in his manner. Two men said they had had a drink with Hanley after work, but that the three of them had split up around seven o'clock and Hanley had not said where he was going. None of his other friends had seen him or talked to him over the weekend, either. One of the former girlfriends they had dredged up had cried. She had been at her sister's wedding that night. The other was a Queens housewife with three small children—and an alibi.

So, it had all come down to the East Side bars, the likeliest places to find out more about what Hanley had done in the hours before his death. But there were so many bars, and most of the people in them were anonymous—and wanted to stay that way. What chance did they have of finding anyone who had seen Ted Hanley that weekend—and would admit to it?

They combed the bars anyway, using the matchbooks they'd found scattered through the apartment as a starting point. They showed Hanley's photo to bartenders, waiters and waitresses, and as many regulars as they could find. A few people said they thought Hanley looked familiar but they couldn't say for sure when they had seen him last.

And then late on Thursday night they hit pay-dirt. They were showing the photo to the bartender in a place in the Sixties. He said he didn't know Hanley at all, so MacLaughlin stuffed the photo back in his wallet and motioned to Gross that they should move on.

As they were walking to the door, a woman sitting at the bar looked them up and down. She was in her early thirties and only marginally attractive.

"Hey, are you cops?" she asked.

"Yeah," MacLaughlin answered gruffly.

"You wouldn't by any chance be checking out that guy Hanley who was murdered, would you?"

The two detectives looked at each other. "Yes, we are," MacLaughlin said quickly. "Did you know him?"

"Yeah, I knew him," she said defiantly. "And believe me, if anyone ever deserved to get it, it was that son of a bitch."

MacLaughlin sat down on the stool next to her and took out his wallet. Gross perched himself on the stool on the other side of her.

MacLaughlin showed her the photo. "Is this the man you're talking about?"

She looked at the snapshot and screwed up her face as if she were going to spit on it. "Yeah, he's the one," she said. "I saw that picture in the paper."

"Then why didn't you call the police?"

"I don't know, I figured I'd get around to it. If I'd known they'd send somebody like you," she said teasingly, "I would have called right away."

MacLaughlin ignored this. He put his wallet back and took out his notebook. "Would you mind telling me your name, miss?"

"Sure. Andrea Pelegrino. You want to know my address?"

MacLaughlin nodded.

"It's two sixty East Sixty-third Street, apartment seven-B. And my phone number is five-five-five one-seven-seven-one." She smiled at him. "Got that?"

"Yeah," he said, not looking up. "What's your date of birth?"

"Why do you want to know that?"

"It's routine."

"Well, it's February 15, 1948," she said testily. "I'm an Aquarius."

MacLaughlin knew she had lied about the year, but he let it pass. "Occupation?"

"Secretary." She gave him the name of a big textile firm.

"How well did you know the victim?"

"Well, I didn't really know him," she said. Then she smiled slyly. "But I *knew* him, if you know what I mean."

MacLaughlin sighed. "Is there anything you can tell us about him that might help in our investigation?"

"Oh, yeah," she said and leaned toward him confidentially. "I think a woman did it. You see, he liked to beat up on women." She searched his face for the desired look of surprise she thought her pronouncement would bring. When it was not forthcoming, she seemed disappointed.

"Yeah," MacLaughlin said. "How do you know?"

"Well, he beat up on *me*," she said, sounding a little hurt. "I should have pressed charges on him."

"Why didn't you?"

"Because I never wanted to *see* that bastard again, that's why."

"What did he do to you?"

"Well, he was real smooth about it, I'll have to say that for him. I met him in a bar a couple of blocks from here, and he seemed so nice at first. I mean, he was really good-looking and he said the right things, so I—" she lowered her eyes a trifle too dramatically, "so I went home with him."

"And then he started beating you up?"

"Not right away. He was still pretty nice, but then he just changed—all of a sudden—it was so strange."

"Did he hit you with anything?"

"Well, he used his hand at first—just to knock me around a few times. But then he hit me with this belt—God, I had bruises on my you-know-what for days."

"Did anything happen after that?"

"No. It was really weird. I mean, he got so crazy, and then he just stopped. After that he was nice again. But I was scared to death of him. I couldn't wait to get out of there. Only he wouldn't let me leave until the next morning."

"When did this happen?"

"Oh, about three or four months ago. During the summer, I think."

"Did you ever see him again?"

"Are you kidding? I would have called you guys if I had."

"Do you know anybody else who might know him?"

"No. If I did, I would have warned them about him."

"Why do you think a woman killed him?" Suspicious now.

"Because it just sounded like it—from the papers, I mean. He was naked, so he had probably been having sex with someone. Well, he must have started beating her up—just like me—and whoever it was got scared, or mad, and killed him. So it must have been a woman—unless he liked guys, too."

MacLaughlin closed his notebook and shot a look at Harry Gross that said, "It's just too easy. Couldn't be." Harry's nod confirmed his thoughts. "Well, thank you very much, Miss Pelegrino. You've been a great help to us. We'll be calling you to come down to the station house to make a formal statement."

"When? Can't I do it right now?"

"I guess so—if you want to," MacLaughlin said uncertainly.

"Sure. Why not? I've got nothing better to do tonight." She called the bartender over and paid her tab. Then she grinned at MacLaughlin. "Let's go," she said, grabbing her coat.

Harry Gross was smirking at his partner. "I think she's going to keep you busy all night, Frank," he whispered to MacLaughlin when she sailed through the door ahead of them.

MacLaughlin shot him a dirty look. "The things I do for this job," he said with a sigh. But still he was glad they had uncovered this woman. She had given them important information. Everything she had said about Ted Hanley—especially the part about the belt, which she couldn't have learned from the papers—had confirmed his theory that

Ted Hanley had brought about his own death. He had liked to beat up on women, and he had finally picked the wrong one. Now, all they had to do was find her.

## CHAPTER SIX

Sandra was dreaming. She was back with Erik, on their honeymoon in Paris—the happiest time of her life. They were strolling down a sunlit boulevard, hand in hand, gazing at people, shop windows, each other. Erik had been so wonderful then. He knew that she had always wanted to see Paris, and this trip had been his special gift to her. But suddenly the brightness of the boulevard was gone and they were in the dim light of the Louvre, looking up at the Venus de Milo. It was so beautiful, but cold, stone cold. Sandra felt herself turn to ice. There was something about the face—something that frightened her. She didn't want to look at it, but couldn't help herself. She stared, fascinated, at the blank, unseeing eyes, the faint smile hovering on the lips, the delicately chiseled nose—features that had suddenly become familiar. Katherine's features. For an instant she stood frozen and then she dropped Erik's hand and started running. He called out to her, but she couldn't turn back. She ran and ran, until she was in a long, narrow gallery. She was still running, so fast that the paintings on the walls sped by in a blur. But there was one, a large painting at the end of the gallery that she could just make out. She was running toward it, and as she drew closer, she could see that it was the figure of a man, nearly naked. She thought the painting must be very old because it looked as though there were cracks across its surface. But as she approached it, she suddenly realized that she knew this painting: it was St. Sebastian, and those weren't cracks in the paint, they were arrows piercing his body, and each arrow had produced a tiny trickle of blood. She stopped abruptly when she came to it, and then tentatively put out her hand to touch his wounds —they were *wet!* She jerked her hand away and stared at it. It was covered with blood. She heard herself screaming. No, that was wrong. *She* hadn't screamed, someone else had. St. Sebastian? No, he was still there, gazing off into heaven with martyred eyes. She heard another scream, and this time she knew that it was coming from somewhere outside her dream.

She sat up in bed, the screams echoing in her ears. How she wished she could drown them out so that their agony wouldn't penetrate every fiber of her being, as they had now every night for nearly a week. If only she could pretend she hadn't heard, she wouldn't have to go in there tonight—again. She could close the door and go back to sleep. But she couldn't. Wearily, she started to get up, then sank back down on the bed. What was the point? It had become like a ritual between them, anyway: she would go into Katherine's room, ask her what was wrong, Katherine would refuse to talk about it and tell her to go back to bed. And she would go, stifling her hurt and anger.

What had happened to their friendship? Katherine was becoming so distant, and Sandra could feel her slipping away. But she didn't know what to do to stop it. Katherine hardly talked to her anymore—except about ordinary, everyday matters. Nothing important. Like what was going on in her mind, what made her wake up screaming every night. Of course, it had to do with Ted's murder—or was there something else?

Whatever it was, it haunted Katherine during the days, too. Because Sandra was not the only one who had noticed the change. That very afternoon Vivian had come to her in the library and asked her what was wrong with Katherine. Naturally, Vivian would be the first person to notice something like that. She had shared an office with Katherine for more than two years now, and before Sandra had come on the scene, she had been Katherine's best friend in the office. Maybe her best friend, period. Katherine still kept in touch with a few of her friends from college and graduate school, but those contacts were only intermittent. No, Vivian and Sandra were the only two people who knew her really well. So it was not surprising that Vivian had noticed the change in her.

What was surprising was that even Stan Herzberg had remarked on it. He had obviously been hanging around Katherine a lot, something Sandra had surmised from the things he said, because Katherine certainly had not told her about it. Twice now he had asked Sandra what was bugging "her friend," because she seemed so "out of it." Sandra had sarcastically remarked that maybe *he* was what was bothering Katherine. He had ignored that and wondered instead whether Katherine had a boyfriend she was having problems with, Sandra had tried to be as vague as possible in her answer—while hinting that he had stumbled onto the truth. Anything to keep him from digging deeper.

How much longer would it be before other people started to notice Katherine's behavior? Maybe they already had. She was deteriorating day by day, and it was a slow and painful process to watch.

Sandra was worried about Katherine, but she had also begun to wonder about herself. She felt rejected, and that depressed her. She had a hard time sleeping, and even when she did get to sleep she had disturbing dreams—usually about Katherine. Of course, her dreams were nothing to rival Katherine's. Sandra could only dimly imagine what those must be to cause her to cry out like that. The sound of sobbing reached her now, and Sandra snuggled down into the bed, pressing the pillow to her ears.

But sleep would not come. Though the muffled sobs gave way to silence, she lay there a long time, thinking about Katherine. And the more she thought, the more upset she became, until she could stand it no longer.

She got up, padded softly to Katherine's door, pushed it open and flipped on the light switch.

Katherine's head jerked up and she squinted at Sandra through the brightness of the light.

"Were you asleep?" Sandra asked.

"No," Katherine mumbled, turning her face away from the light.

"I've got to talk to you," Sandra said. "Or—more to the point—I want *you* to talk to me." Instead of sitting on the edge of the bed as she usually did, she pulled the chair out from Katherine's desk, put it next to the bed, and sat down.

Katherine's eyes had a guarded look as she pushed herself up to a sitting position. "What do you want me to talk about?"

"Don't do that to me," Sandra implored her. "I heard you again tonight, and I promised myself I wouldn't come in here. But"—she gestured helplessly with her hands—"I couldn't go back to sleep because I was worrying about you. This can't go on any longer, Katherine. You've *got* to tell me what's making you behave so—so strangely." Her eyes were fixed on Katherine's face.

Katherine looked away from the intensity of Sandra's gaze. "No," she said simply. "I know this can't go on. I've been lying here, trying to figure out what to do, and I've decided—I'm going to go see my shrink."

"Oh." The words had struck Sandra like a blow, but she strained to keep her voice impassive. "Do you think that's wise?"

Katherine shot her a look out of the corner of her eye. "Why not?"

"Well, it scares me, for one thing," Sandra said, biting her lip. "And I guess it hurts me a little, too. It makes me feel shut out, like you don't trust me. We're in this thing together, and I feel that it's *me*

you should be coming to for help—not some
shrink."

Katherine's gaze softened. "I *do* trust you, Sandra. It's just—"

"What?"

"Nothing." Katherine dismissed this with a
wave of her hand. Then her eyes narrowed slightly.
"Why would it scare you for me to see my shrink?"

Sandra frowned. "Because it's too many people
knowing, that's why."

"But I wouldn't talk about *him*," Katherine said
quickly.

Sandra looked puzzled. "But—how could you
avoid it? Isn't that why you want to go?"

Katherine looked away. "No," she said hesitantly. "Th-that's not exactly it." There was a faint
glimmer of tears in her eyes.

Sandra wanted to comfort her. She moved to
the edge of the chair. "Katherine, please," she said
softly, reaching out to touch Katherine's hand.
"Let me help you."

Suddenly Katherine gripped Sandra's hand. She
could hold back the tears no longer, and they came
in a rush. "N—nobody can help me," she said
through her sobs.

Sandra put her other hand around Katherine's
and squeezed it. "No!" she said. "That's not true!
I'm your friend, and I care about you and want
to help you. But I can't if you don't tell me what's
wrong."

"I can't!" Katherine sobbed, jerking her head
violently from side to side. "I can't!"

Sandra wrenched her hands away from Katherine's, sprang to the bed, and took Katherine in

her arms. Katherine buried her face against Sandra's shoulder. She let the sobs come freely, huge spasms that shook her whole body. Sandra rocked her back and forth, as if she were a child.

Katherine continued to cry hysterically, and Sandra held her like that for a long time. After several minutes she became conscious of a wet warm feeling above her breast where Katherine's tears had penetrated the thin cloth of her nightgown. The tears were warm and made the cloth cling to her skin, and she suddenly remembered a time when she was thirteen and had gone walking in the summer rain with a boy. Her blouse had gotten wet and transparent, and she had found the cloth sticking to her body strangely exciting. When the boy had awkwardly tried to feel her breasts she had let him.

She began stroking Katherine's dark head and was startled by a movement across the room. She looked up and saw her own reflection in the mirror above Katherine's dresser. At first she almost did not recognize herself—she had such a serene, Madonna-like expression on her face. She studied it thoughtfully and then suppressed a smile. If only Erik could see that face, he would say, "I told you so!" and wax ecstatic about women having a natural instinct for motherhood. Maybe he's right, she thought, if being a mother means being needed. Because this is what she had wanted all along —for Katherine to need her.

At last, when Katherine's sobs had diminished, Sandra asked, "Do you feel better now?" She felt Katherine's head nod feebly in response. "Good," she said gently. "Now, don't you think you'd better try talking to me? Look what it's doing to you. You can't keep it inside any longer."

Katherine slowly pushed away. Her nose was running and her eyes were all puffy. "I need a tissue," she said helplessly.

Sandra handed her one from the table by the bed. Katherine wiped her eyes with it and then blew her nose. She looked dolefully at Sandra. "I guess you're right," she said in an uneven, breathy voice. "But it's so hard."

"Then just take it one step at a time," Sandra said. "You've got all night—we're obviously not going to get any sleep."

Katherine managed a weak smile. "No, I guess not." She dabbed at her eyes again and then wadded up the wet tissue in her hand.

Sandra handed her another tissue and moved back to the chair, letting Katherine pull herself together.

Katherine blew her nose again. She seemed reluctant to speak, and yet determined to get it over with. "It's—I really don't know where to start—because it's been happening for so long." She tore off a piece of tissue and wrapped it around her index finger, twisting and untwisting it. "I—I guess," she said at last, "that I should tell you about the nightmares. Except, there's really only one. You see," she looked at Sandra, agony twisting her face, "they're almost always the same."

"My God," Sandra said. "How long has this been going on?"

Katherine took a deep breath. "I remember the first one," she said. "Very distinctly. It was the night my father beat me up for the first time. I was just eleven then, really only a child, and the nightmare frightened me so that I woke up screaming my head off. My mother came running into my room, and I tried to tell her about the nightmare—but then I saw my father standing in the doorway. And I got scared and told her that I had dreamt about some monster I saw on a TV show. She laughed and told me I was being silly and I shouldn't worry about such things because they weren't real. And then I forgot about it—until the next time my father beat me up." She paused for a moment, lost in the memories of how her father had looked at her body, at the tiny breasts showing on her once-flat chest. He had made her feel dirty when he looked at her like that, so she knew she had done something wrong. Then he had started to hit her—across her back, buttocks and thighs—at first with his fist and then with his belt. But she had been so confused because she couldn't remember exactly what it was she had done to deserve such punishment.

"When did that happen?" Sandra prodded her gently back to the present.

Katherine tugged at the tissue on her finger. "Oh, maybe a couple of months later. When he did it again, I had the nightmare again. Only this time my parents were out, but my brother was home from school and he heard me screaming. When I told him I had a nightmare, he laughed at me and called me a baby. He was fourteen then and I guess he didn't mean to be cruel, he just wanted to sound like a big man—like my father,

I suppose. But what he said hurt me, and I think that had a lot to do with why I never told anyone about my nightmares ever again."

Sandra's brow furrowed. "But you told *me* you had them."

Katherine's eyes met hers evenly. "You're the only one."

"You mean you didn't tell your shrink?"

Katherine shook her head. "Not even her—I could never bring myself to do it. It was hard enough to tell her about my father beating me up. Maybe if I'd been able to stick with therapy I'd have told her eventually . . ." Her voice drifted off.

"Tell me," Sandra said, cutting into her thoughts, "did you only have the nightmares whenever your father beat you up?"

Katherine sighed. "At first, yes. But then things changed and I started having them at other times. I guess as I got older, I got angrier and angrier with him. Whenever he'd try to hit me, I'd fight back. That only made him madder, and I knew it. But I couldn't help it, I couldn't just passively let him take out all his frustrations on me." She smiled, almost proudly. "Once, I even managed to scratch his face."

"My God! Didn't your mother notice that?"

"Of course. But she never said anything about it—not in front of me, anyway. He probably told her he cut it shaving, and she didn't want to push it—maybe she was afraid she'd find out he had a girlfriend."

"Was she afraid of him, too?"

"Not of him, no—but she was afraid of rocking the boat. You see, I think my mother has always felt a little inferior. She comes from a well-to-do family in the Midwest, but they don't have nearly the status that my father's family does—all they have is money. His family has that, too, but they also have this *name*. You know, they came over on the *Mayflower* and all that. So when my father deigned to give my mother that name, he gave her something that all her money could never buy. Because of that, she would never do anything that might displease him. For instance, when he started beating me up I begged her to send me away to boarding school. At first, she was all for it, but when my father refused, she backed down immediately."

"But couldn't she *see*—I mean, how did you act toward your father when she was around?"

"Like nothing had happened. I was afraid of what he would do to me if I acted any other way. And then I just tried to make myself scarce whenever he was around."

"I don't know," Sandra said, shaking her head. "I just don't understand your parents." In the newspaper picture they had looked so—so elegant and so *refined*.

Katherine shrugged. "I don't understand it either. I suppose they're nice enough—I mean on the surface. They have beautiful manners and they know how to treat people like servants and friends. They're just rotten parents."

"I hope I never meet them."

Katherine scowled. "You don't have to worry about that."

"But it would be interesting," Sandra mused. "Especially when I know all their little secrets."

"No," Katherine said harshly. "I don't ever want that to happen." She looked quickly away.

Sandra's eyebrows lifted a little, but then she leaned forward. "Tell me more about the nightmares," she said. "Didn't you say before that your father stopped beating you up when you went to college? Did the nightmares stop then, too?"

Katherine nodded. "Yes, they did. It was funny, because before I went to Smith I was so worried that I wouldn't be able to stay there because I'd wake everybody up with my screaming. But they stopped. Just like that." She snapped her fingers. "I was so happy. I felt *normal* for the first time in years. Even when I went home for vacations there was no problem. And my father never laid a hand on me again." She dropped her eyes to the tissue on her finger and twisted it until it was pinching her skin. "But when I left school," she said in an odd, tight voice, "the nightmares came back . . ."

Sandra waited for Katherine to speak again. When she didn't, she asked as gently as she could, "Can you tell me about them?"

Katherine had retreated back into her shell. She gave Sandra a long, suspicious look. "Why are they so important to you?"

"What?" Sandra said, taken aback.

Katherine set her jaw. "I want to know why you're trying to dig all this out of me."

Sandra shook her head sadly. She stood up. "Haven't we been through all that?" she said wearily. Then the anger and hurt surfaced. "All right," she cried, shouting now, "*don't* tell me. Go on torturing yourself night and day. Or go to your goddamn shrink! Only I'm not going to be around anymore to take this kind of crap!" And she started walking toward the door.

Katherine sat bolt upright. "Where are you going?"

Sandra turned slowly and looked at her. "For now, to bed. Tomorrow I think I'd better start looking for another apartment."

"No!" Katherine leaped out of bed and grabbed Sandra's arm. "Please," she begged, her face twisted with pain, "*please* don't leave me. You're all I've got—you're the only one who cares. I don't know what I'd do without you."

Sandra stared at her. "That's right, Katherine," she said coldly. "I *am* the only one who cares about you. But you're so wrapped up in yourself that you can't see that it hurts *me* to be shut out, to see you going through hell—and not know why."

Katherine looked at her for what seemed like an eternity. Then she threw her arms around Sandra and hugged her. "My God," she said, "you really *are* my friend."

Sandra's arms hung limply at her sides. Katherine's response was so unexpected that she did not know quite what to make of it.

Katherine drew back and looked earnestly at Sandra. "I'll tell you now," she said. "*Everything.* I *want* to tell you." She gently pushed Sandra toward the chair. "Please, sit down and listen to me."

Sandra sat on the edge of the chair and looked quizzically at Katherine.

Katherine sat on the bed, arms circling her knees. She looked penitent. "I don't know why I said that before," she said. "Maybe I'm afraid to tell you because I'm afraid you'll hate me afterward. I'm really sorry. Can you forgive me?"

Sandra bent her head. "Of course, I can." Then she looked up. "Don't worry about me. I could *never* hate you."

Katherine sighed deeply. "Yeah, well, maybe." She rubbed her hand across her forehead. "When I've told you everything, I want you to tell me what you think—the truth."

"I'll try—that's all I can promise."

"I guess I can't ask for any more than that," Katherine said, and drew herself up as if trying to gather her courage before she spoke again. "As I said before," she began hesitantly, "the awful thing about the nightmares is that they're almost always the same. I—" her voice quivered, "I'm standing in a room. No place special, just a room. Then the door opens and this man walks in—my father—and he comes over to me. He's upset and he tells me that he needs my help. I don't do anything, I just stand there—looking at him. And then he starts pleading with me, *begging* me to help him. It makes me laugh to see him like that. Because I'm laughing at him, he gets very sad and starts crying. That only makes me laugh all the more. So then he looks very hurt and dejected and turns to walk away. But he only goes a couple of steps because I suddenly have this knife in my hand and I—I—"

"You don't have to say anymore," Sandra cut in. "I can guess the rest."

"No!" Katherine cried. "I've got to say it! I stab

him—in the back—again and again, until he's dead!"

Sandra was afraid that Katherine would start crying again. But she was beyond that. Her eyes, still red from before, burned brightly as she searched Sandra's face for a reaction.

"Is that when you wake up screaming?" Sandra asked softly.

Katherine nodded mutely.

Sandra reached out to touch her arm. "I can see why you've been so upset. It's too much like what really happened—with Ted."

Katherine shuddered. "S—sometimes I see *him* in the nightmares, instead of my father. And he —he looks at me as he's dying. Just like he did that night." She covered her eyes with her hand. "That look—oh, God—I can never forget it."

Sandra gripped her arm. "But, Katherine, don't you understand? He was a monster. He *deserved* to die. He was a vicious sadist and he *enjoyed* beating me up. Didn't you see it on his face? Anybody who does things like that is *asking* for it."

Katherine took her hand away from her eyes and looked thoughtfully at Sandra. "Then you don't think that I'm really a—a—?"

"A murderer?" Sandra shook her head solemnly. "No. Sure, you dreamt about killing your father— that isn't so crazy. It was only natural for you to hate him. Look what he did to you."

Katherine's voice wavered. "I don't know. I want to believe you. You make it all sound so rational."

"Look," Sandra said, trying to keep herself calm, "you've been through a lot. What happened to you —to us—with Ted was horrible, and you're feeling guilty about it. But the fact that it was so much like your nightmares is sheer coincidence."

Katherine seemed heartened. "Yes, I suppose it could be—and I tried to tell myself it was, at first." Then her face fell. "But the nightmares got worse and worse, and it got to the point where I couldn't tell the difference between the nightmares and what really happened. And then I started wondering whether or not I really meant to— *wanted* to—kill Ted."

"That's absurd. You did it because you *had* to. If you hadn't stopped him, who knows what he would have done?"

"That's true, isn't it?" Katherine said fervently. "And I wasn't thinking of myself then—I was thinking of *you*."

"That's right," Sandra said. "You did it to protect me."

Sandra's heart leaped. This was the moment she had been waiting for, to hear Katherine admit how much she cared for her. "That's right," she repeated gently. "You did it for me." Her hand was still resting on Katherine's arm, and unaware of what she was doing, she loosened her grip until it was more like a tender caress. "Is that because you love me?" she whispered, stroking Katherine's arm.

Horrified, Katherine stared down at the hand fondling her arm. "What are you doing?" she asked hoarsely.

Sandra jerked her hand away from Katherine's arm as if it were on fire. "Nothing," she said, feeling ashamed. "I—I'm sorry—"

"I'm tired," Katherine said, turning away from her. "I'm going to sleep."

Sandra got up, hurt and confused, and afraid of her own emotions. "Katherine—" she said tentatively.

"Just go to bed," Katherine said, biting off the words scornfully.

Sandra paused in the doorway. She started to speak again, but the words died on her lips when she saw the cold, withdrawn look on Katherine's face. She turned and ran to her own room, her eyes brimming with tears, and her heart filled with hate.

## CHAPTER SEVEN

Philip Fielding's listing in *Who's Who* was twenty-four lines long. Sandra had counted them.

This was not the first time she had looked him up in the reference volume, but the first time it had merely been out of idle curiosity sparked by a society page photo of two chic-looking people named Fielding. Almost as a joke, she had asked Katherine if she was related to them. Katherine had blanched and replied stiffly, "Yes, they're my parents," and rapidly changed the subject. Sandra had been astounded. And she had gone to the reference materials in the library and looked Philip Fielding up.

This time her intentions were much more serious. She had just called Katherine and found out she was working frantically on a story that had to go out that afternoon. Certain there was no chance she would appear in the library, Sandra then went to *Who's Who* and read through the cut-and-dried facts of Philip Fielding's life again. They were all there: his birthplace and date; his parents' names; all his schools and degrees; his wife's name and the date of their marriage; his children's names (including Katherine's middle name, Hatcher);

all his positions and accomplishments as a lawyer; and his business and home addresses. But who was the man behind all those degrees, honors, titles? That was what Sandra really wanted to know.

She only knew two other things about him than what was given in *Who's Who:* that he was dark and handsome, and that he had a secret, vicious temper.

Sandra's preoccupation with Philip Fielding had been building since Katherine had revealed the content of her nightmares. She couldn't exactly say why she was so fascinated by the man, except that she knew it had something to do with the two opposing images she had of him in her mind: a rich, cultivated aristocrat and a violent, vengeful father who had savagely beaten his beautiful, defenseless daughter. How could one man be both things?

Sandra slammed *Who's Who* shut and put it back on the shelf. Then she closed the library door and locked it. She always locked the door whenever she was gone for any length of time; if anyone saw it shut now they would assume she was on an errand and would come back later.

She got out the Yellow Pages and riffled through it until she found the listing for "Lawyers." When she found Philip Fielding's number, she dialed it with shaking fingers. A crisp female voice answered. She panicked and hung up, chiding herself for being such a coward. She waited several minutes and dialed again. Why am I doing this? she wondered as the first ring sounded. The switchboard operator picked up immediately and Sandra felt her mouth go dry. "I'd like to speak to Mr. Fielding." The voice was not hers, but a hoarse whisper.

"Just a moment, please." Click.

Another click. "Mr. Fielding's office. Mrs. Porter speaking."

"I'd like to speak to Mr. Fielding, please," Sandra heard herself say in a rush. "My name is Sandra Jurgenson. He doesn't know me, but I'm a friend of his daughter's. It's a personal matter."

"Hold on, please." Click.

Her head was spinning. Why didn't she just hang up now?

Click. "Hello, Miss Jurgenson," a resonant, masculine voice said. "This is Philip Fielding. What can I do for you?"

"M—Mr. Fielding, I'm Katherine's roommate—"

"Oh, yes," he said graciously. "Katherine's mentioned you."

Like hell she has, Sandra thought. But he had said it with such charm that she wanted to believe it. His smoothness, the deep, soft voice left her momentarily speechless.

"Is Katherine all right?" Mr. Fielding asked quickly. "I haven't talked to her recently."

Does he really care, Sandra wondered, or is he just showing good form? "Well, that's what I called about," she said. "I'm sure it's nothing really, but Katherine has been having some, uh, problems lately—"

"What kind of problems?"

The voice was sharper now. Sandra was sure

that she had caught an edge of fear in it. What was he afraid of? "It's nothing to be alarmed about," she went on quickly, trying to sound reassuring. "I just thought that you and Mrs. Fielding ought to know, and I didn't think that Katherine would tell you herself."

"Yes, that's right," he said. "My daughter is a very independent young woman."

"I know," Sandra said.

"Yes, I suppose you do," he laughed.

Sandra was surprised by the depth of emotion his ironic laughter held. Suddenly, she was not quite so afraid of him.

"Mr. Fielding," she said, "I don't really want to talk about this over the phone. I know you're a busy man, but would it be possible for you to see me sometime?"

"Yes, of course, Miss Jurgenson. What time is best for you?"

"Well, lunch hour is the only time I can really get away."

"Fine. Excuse me for a moment while I check with my secretary." Click.

Sandra still couldn't quite believe how smoothly this was going.

Click. "Miss Jurgenson?"

"Yes."

"I have lunch free tomorrow. Would that be all right with you?"

"Yes, that's fine." She'd tell Katherine she had to go to the doctor or something.

"Would you like me to send a car for you?"

A car? Sandra gulped. She wanted to say yes,

but the image of a big, black limousine sitting in front of her office building, stopped her. What if somebody saw her? "Oh, no," she said quickly. "That won't be necessary."

"All right. Shall we say twelve thirty?"

"Fine." That meant she'd have to leave at twelve, since it would take her about half an hour on the subway.

"I hope you'll have lunch with me?"

"Oh, that would be very nice." In that case, she'd have to take some extra time, tell Mrs. Morgan, her supervisor, that she had a doctor's appointment and arrange for someone to take over the library until she got back.

"Good. Do you know where my office is?"

"Wall Street?"

"Yes. Number 250. Just a few doors down from Federal Hall. Thirtieth floor. I'm looking forward to meeting you, Miss Jurgenson."

"Thank you. I'm looking forward to meeting you, too." And how.

"See you tomorrow then. Good-bye."

"Good-bye."

Sandra put the receiver back in its cradle and let out a sigh. She had pulled it off. Well, almost. She still had to get through tomorrow.

Sandra had not liked lying to Katherine. Lying to Mrs. Morgan had been easy because Sandra considered her the kind of tough old lady who would have cheerfully chained all her underlings to their desks if slavery hadn't been abolished.

But looking into Katherine's eyes this morning

on the bus and lying about where she was going for her lunch hour today had pricked her conscience.

All that was behind her now, though, as she hurried toward Grand Central and the subway. Her feet followed the route automatically, even though her body was dragging slightly behind. But her mind—where was it?—was somewhere else: back at her desk, out to lunch with Katherine, anywhere but here, rushing down Madison Avenue to an appointment with what? Destiny? No, that was silly and melodramatic. She was merely going to meet her best friend's father. She'd met fathers of her friends before. Why should this be any different? But it was—and she knew it.

As she strode across the huge, vaulted lobby of Grand Central, she glanced at the clock. 12:08. She had plenty of time, as long as she could get a train right away. A few more yards and she plunged down the steps to the subway entrance. She could hear a train coming in, so she fished a token out of her coat pocket, slipped it into the turnstile slot, pushed through, and dashed to the steps leading to the downtown trains. An express had just pulled in. She bolted down the steps and ran through the closest set of doors. Just in time—the doors closed behind her, and she collapsed into the nearest seat. A well-dressed man sitting directly across from her looked up, gave her the once-over, and then went back to his *Wall Street Journal*.

Sandra caught her breath as the train shook and rattled its way into the tunnel. Faster and faster it went, passing all the local stops. Her mind was racing along with it, asking herself *Why am I doing this?* But the only answer she could give was, *I don't know. I really don't know.*

Maybe it was like wanting to see a movie star or a celebrity in person, she thought. Yes, that could be it. Somehow, seeing or touching or talking to someone who was larger-than-life added to your own life, made you feel as important as they. Or maybe it cut them down more to your size.

And yet she was terrified of meeting this man, but even more frightened of what Katherine would do if she found out.

But that hadn't stopped her. She felt almost— driven. There was something inside her that was pushing her forward, making her will the train to go faster.

The stations went rushing by until suddenly Wall Street was the next stop. Clutching her purse to her side, she stood up, carefully balancing herself, and walked slowly to the doors. Gripping a pole, she braced herself for the lurching stop, and sprang through the doors as they opened, her eyes already searching for the exit as she stepped onto the platform. As she pressed through the turnstile and began to climb the steps, she stifled a feeling of panic: What if she got lost? What if she couldn't find his office? This area was practically foreign to her, and the people rushing around her looked unfriendly, too busy to be bothered giving directions.

She paused at the top of the stairs and got her bearings, feeling as she had when she had first come to the city. Whenever she came out of the subway she had always been confused, without any sense of direction.

Then she spotted Trinity Church. That was her landmark. Wall Street would be just opposite it. She headed in that direction, her confidence returning, past the imposing bulk of the New York Stock Exchange, past the Greek Revival Federal Hall with its statue of George Washington. Just a few more steps . . .

Yes, there it was. Number 250. It was an old building, almost genteel, with just the right amount of ornate decor gracing the lobby. She expected to find an elevator operator as she stepped into the car, but no, it was self-service. She touched the button for the thirtieth floor. The doors silently closed and the car moved upward.

Glad she was alone in the elevator, Sandra took a small mirror out of her purse and checked her makeup—again. Was it too much? No, in fact, she looked rather demure. She ran a comb through her hair, unbuttoned her coat, and smoothed out the pale wool fabric of her dress.

The elevator stopped, the doors glided open, and Sandra stepped out into a hushed corridor. She licked her lips nervously as she stared at the small, discreet sign facing the elevator: Fielding, Redmond & Turner, Suite 3001. There was an arrow pointing to the right.

She looked at her watch as she opened the large, paneled door of Suite 3001. 12:29. Right on time. Her eyes barely took in the deep, dark wood paneling of the reception area, the Persian rug or the leather chairs as she walked over to the receptionist's desk. Austere-looking, almost forbidding, the receptionist seemed to be appraising Sandra until her face broke into a professional smile. "May I help you?"

"Yes." Sandra hoped that the woman didn't notice the quiver in her voice. "I'm here to see Philip Fielding. My name is Sandra Jurgenson."

"Just a moment, Miss Jurgenson," the woman said, gesturing toward the leather chairs. "Won't you have a seat while you're waiting?" She picked up the phone and dialed a number.

Sandra obediently sat on the closest chair. Trying to appear nonchalant under the receptionist's hovering eyes, she picked up a magazine from a nearby table and leafed through it. Her heart was pounding so loud that she couldn't hear what the receptionist was saying into the phone.

"Miss Jurgenson," the receptionist said, hanging up, "Mr. Fielding's secretary will be out in just a moment."

"Thank you," Sandra said, and she tried to smile, but the muscles in her face and throat were so constricted that she could barely feel them move. She started to swallow, but felt herself gagging instead. *Oh, my God, I'm going to choke to death right here in his office,* Sandra thought, and she wondered whether she dared ask the receptionist for a glass of water.

Just then a striking, middle-aged woman appeared and walked purposefully toward her.

"Miss Jurgenson?"

Sandra nodded.

"I'm Mrs. Porter, Mr. Fielding's secretary. Won't you come with me, please?"

Somehow Sandra managed to get to her feet.

She followed Mrs. Porter around a corner and down a corridor.

Over her shoulder Mrs. Porter said, "I'm afraid Mr. Fielding is tied up on an overseas call right now, but he should be off shortly."

Sandra mumbled something to show that she understood.

"This way," Mrs. Porter said, and turned through a door to the right. "May I take your coat?" she asked.

Sandra took off her coat and handed it to her. "Have a seat, please," she said. "It'll just be a moment, I'm sure."

Sandra sat down and took in Mrs. Porter's office. It was nearly as big as Charles's, she thought, but furnished with elegant-looking antiques and more like a study than an office. There was only one visible piece of office equipment—the typewriter.

In spite of her businesslike black suit, Mrs. Porter looked more like an upper-class matron than a secretary. She had thick, steely-gray hair that framed the soft roundness of her face, but her eyes had a kind of cool detachment when she spoke.

"I understand you're a friend of Katherine's," she said, trying to make conversation.

"Yes, I am," Sandra said. "I'm her roommate."

"How nice. How *is* Katherine? I haven't seen her for such a long time."

"Oh, she's fine."

"Good. Katherine is such a beautiful—" She was stopped short by the sound of a buzzer. "Excuse me," she said to Sandra as she pressed the intercom button on the phone. "Yes?" she said into the receiver. "Yes. I'll be right in." She got up from her desk. "Mr. Fielding will see you in just a moment," she said, and disappeared through a door to Sandra's left.

Sandra's palms were sweaty and she foraged in her purse for a tissue to wipe them off. She couldn't find one so she rubbed her hands across the upholstered surface of her chair.

The door swung open and Sandra's heart leapt. "Miss Jurgenson," Mrs. Porter said, standing in the doorway, "Mr. Fielding will see you now."

Sandra pushed herself up from the chair and held her breath as she walked across the room. Mrs. Porter was holding the door and smiling at her, but Sandra could not get her face to work right to smile back.

The room was huge—as big as their whole apartment—two walls were almost entirely windows, and the light flooding in was so bright that she had to blink after the softer lamplight of Mrs. Porter's office. The walls were paneled in rosewood and lined with bookshelves filled with thick, leather-bound volumes. Three Persian rugs covered the glossy parquet floor and divided the room into sections, one for his desk, another for a conversation area with a couch and two big chairs, and a third for a long conference table. His desk was massive, made of finely carved dark wood that glowed with the patina of many years of loving care.

He stood up and came round his desk. His dark hair was touched with gray at the temples and his face had a few lines in it, but other than that he could have passed for Katherine's twin brother.

He was tall, over six feet, and his trim, graceful body was set off by an impeccably tailored gray pinstripe suit and vest. The gray in the suit perfectly matched the soft gray of his eyes. The newspaper picture had not done him justice. He was one of the handsomest men she had ever seen.

"How do you do, Miss Jurgenson," he was saying. "I'm so pleased to meet you." He extended his hand.

Sandra shook it. She was unable to speak, but forced the corners of her mouth up into a frozen grin.

"Please, sit down," he said, indicating the couch. "I think you'll be more comfortable there."

With an effort, she tore her eyes away from him, sat down, and pretended to be looking out the windows.

"What do you think of my view?" he asked, taking a chair facing her.

"Oh, it's spectacular," Sandra responded, suddenly conscious of what it was she was seeing. Except for a few taller buildings in the way, the window commanded a panorama of the entire harbor.

"You should have seen it when I first moved in here," Mr. Fielding said, "before they put up those buildings. It was breathtaking. I especially enjoyed watching the great liners moving in and out of the harbor. That was thrilling."

"Yes, I can imagine," Sandra said, letting her eyes wander back to his face again. It was almost painful for her to look at him. Not only because he was so handsome but because he was such a nearly perfect masculine version of Katherine.

He was smiling at her, and Sandra couldn't tell if it was a genuine smile or just his way of showing her that he was waiting for her to tell him why she had come.

She took a deep breath. Might as well make the plunge. "Well, I suppose you're wondering why I wanted to talk to you." She hated the tenuous sound of her own voice.

"Yes, I am rather curious." The smile had disappeared and been replaced by a look of concern.

"I don't exactly know how to put this—" *Then stop dallying and get to the point!* "But I think Katherine may be on the verge of—having a nervous breakdown." There, it was out.

His eyes narrowed almost imperceptibly. "What makes you think that?"

Sandra hesitated. "Well, it's several things," she said, unable to meet his piercing gaze. It was amazing how much alike they were, a likeness that went beyond the physical. They had the same way of leveling their clear gray eyes at you so that they seemed to be hanging on your every word, the same way of appearing to consider and discard several words in a split second before they found just the right one to say to you.

"Please. Tell me what they are," he said earnestly.

"Maybe it's nothing—but she's not sleeping well. She has horrible nightmares that wake her up almost every night, and she seems distracted during the day. She's fallen behind in her work, so I'm not the only one who's noticed it."

Leaning his elbows on the arms of his chair, he pressed the tips of his fingers together and studied them at length before he spoke. "How long has this been going on?"

"About three weeks now."

He nodded, twisted in his chair to face the windows to his left, and stared out at the view. Sandra could only see his face in profile, but it looked drawn. "Do you think she needs professional help?" he asked finally, turning back to look at her.

"I don't know," Sandra hedged. "I'm not really qualified to judge that. I've talked to her about it, but she seems reluctant to try it. But she told me she did see someone—a few years ago."

He nodded. "Yes, she—" He broke off and quickly passed his hand over his eyes. "There were some . . . problems about eight or nine years ago. But I thought all that was over with."

Sandra didn't know what he was talking about, but she kept still.

"I know Katherine doesn't like me to interfere." He paused. When he continued, his voice had a new intensity. "I love my daughter very much," he said, looking directly at Sandra. "But she doesn't—she won't talk to me—" He looked away, his hands gripping the arms of his chair so tightly that the knuckles were white. Then the spasm of emotion passed, and he looked back at Sandra. "Do you think it would help if her mother talked to her?" he asked.

Sandra stiffened. "No," she said quickly. "Please don't do that. You see, she doesn't know that I came to see you."

"Yes, I gathered that," Philip Fielding said with a slightly sardonic note in his voice.

"Actually, I don't think anybody should do anything just yet—not until Katherine asks for help."

Mr. Fielding sighed. "Yes, but knowing Katherine, she won't do that unless she's absolutely forced to."

Sandra shook her head. "No, I don't think that'll happen. She'll listen to me eventually—I'll make her."

Mr. Fielding studied her face for a moment. "I'm glad Katherine has a friend like you," he said. There was an odd mixture of pain and gratitude in his voice.

Sandra lowered her eyes. "She's been a good friend to me, too," she said almost shyly.

He leaned forward. "You say that she's fallen behind in her work. Is there any danger of her losing her job?"

Sandra looked up at him. "I don't know," she said. "She's really respected there—although she's not entirely appreciated."

"If she lost her job, that would be quite a blow to her."

"Yes—yes, it would."

"I'm sure Katherine hasn't told you this," he said in confidential tones, "but she doesn't need to work—not for money, anyway. She inherited trust funds from both her mother's family and mine, but I don't think she's ever touched them. Instead, she has insisted on living off what she makes. I used to think she was being foolish, but now I rather admire her for it."

"Oh," Sandra said, shocked. "No, I didn't know that." She suddenly felt embarrassed, remembering how she had used financial expedience as a means of pressuring Katherine into sharing the apartment with her.

He settled back in his chair. "So, Miss Jurgenson, for the time being you suggest we do nothing?"

"Well, yes," Sandra said. "But I wanted you to be aware of what was happening, just in case."

"I'm grateful to you," he said. "And I'd like you to keep me informed. For the time being, I think we'll just keep this between you and me. I won't say anything to Mrs. Fielding. I wouldn't want to worry her unnecessarily."

"No, I suppose not," Sandra said. "And I promise I will let you know if anything happens."

"Good," he said. He fell silent for a few moments, and when he continued, his voice had regained its smooth, almost professional tone. "And now I propose that we drop the subject and concentrate on something more pleasant. Would you like to have lunch now?"

"Yes, whatever you say."

"Fine. I thought that instead of dining here in the midst of all these dreary legal types, you might like to go to the restaurant at the World Trade Center. Have you been there?"

"No, I haven't—but I've always wanted to."

"Wonderful," he said. "It's quite a clear day, so I think you will enjoy the view—it's even better than mine. And the food is rather good, too."

He was turning her head. She hadn't expected to be treated quite this royally.

Sandra was only vaguely aware of her surroundings as she walked along the street with him. But she did notice the stares and admiring glances of passers-by, and wondered if people thought they were a couple. For a moment she luxuriated in fantasizing that they were.

He was talking to her about the history of the area, pointing out various sites of interest as they passed them, and she was trying to look attentive. But his nearness was distracting. Was she imagining it, or did he really have an almost tangible aura of power and wealth about him?

His overcoat was of camel's hair cashmere, and she just knew that if she touched it the fabric would feel exquisitely soft under her fingers. Surreptitiously she slipped off a glove, and in the jostling lunchtime crowd managed to brush her bare hand up against his sleeve. It felt like velvet.

As they crossed the street, he put his hand under her arm and gently guided her through the traffic and inside the North Tower. She could feel the strength in his gloved hand, even through her coat, and it made her spine tingle.

But while the elevator was making its dizzying ascent to the one-hundred-and-seventh floor she suddenly had a terrifying thought: Heights always made her queasy. What if she got sick and embarrassed herself at lunch?

He must have seen the dismay in her face because he leaned over to her. "I don't care much for this ride myself," he said reassuringly. "They say it only takes fifty-eight seconds, but I'd rather travel a little slower and arrive with my stomach intact."

Sandra smiled up at him.

The elevator came to a stop, the doors opened, and suddenly they were in a world apart, where everything was beautiful, serene, elegant. Sandra tried not to gawk at the picture-postcard view, the luxurious appointments of the restaurant, the obviously exclusive clientele, and yet she felt that he expected her to. He would not have brought her here if he weren't trying to impress her.

She was aware that the restaurant was a club for-members-only during lunch, and she could see he was well-known and respected. Immediately they were ushered to a table by the windows.

It was one of those rare days in New York when the air is crisp and clean. She forgot all about her fear of heights as she picked out Washington Square Park, the Empire State and Pan Am buildings, and, just beyond them, her own office building on Madison Avenue. How small and insignificant it appeared from here. Off in the distance, tiny planes swept into the sky as they took off from La Guardia. This was New York as she had dreamed of it in far-off Minneapolis.

She let him order for them both and he seemed flattered. She did not really taste the food that was set before her, or the wine, except that she was sure she had too much of that. Was it the wine or the height that was making her so giddy, or was it being with this man in this special place where she could look down on everyone? But what gave her the headiest feeling of all was her own secret power over Philip Fielding. She could completely destroy this man and his world with one sentence: "Your darling Katherine has killed a man." She would not say those words, but she didn't have to. Just knowing that she could was enough.

As he was signing the check, he looked up at her. "I hope you'll let me send you back in the car."

"Oh, no, I'd better not," she mumbled.

"I see," he laughed. "It might give rise to some rumors if you were dropped off at your office in a limousine."

Sandra blushed. "Mmm, that's true."

"Well, I'll tell you what," he said. "Why don't we have the chauffeur let you out a couple of blocks away?"

"I—I guess that would be okay," Sandra managed to stammer.

"Good," he said. "I'll call for the car."

It was waiting for them when they reached the street—all big, black and shiny, with a uniformed chauffeur who jumped to attention and opened the door for Sandra. Mr. Fielding instructed the driver, then turned to Sandra. "I want to thank you for a most pleasant lunch," he said. "I can't tell you what a relief it was for me not to have to talk business." He took her hand in his and lowered his voice. "And I want you to know how grateful I am for what you told me. Please call me in a few days and let me know how everything is. I'll be only too happy to hear from you. And if there's anything I can do, don't hesitate to ask."

"Thank you," Sandra said. "I'll remember that. I just hope it won't be necessary."

"Yes, I do, too," he said, shaking her hand. "Good-bye. It was such a pleasure meeting you. Don't forget to call."

"No, I won't," Sandra said. "Good-bye, and thank you for lunch."

"You're quite welcome." He helped her into the car. He shut the door and waved at her, and Sandra smiled back at him. As the big car pulled away from the curb she glanced back over her shoulder and was startled to see how old he suddenly looked. He had been keeping up a façade for her, Sandra realized. He must be worrying about Katherine. How sad. He really loves her, and she hates him.

She leaned back against the plush upholstery. Surely Katherine had lied about her father—or at least exaggerated. The man was just not capable of the savagery Katherine had described—not unless he was provoked. And she had hurt him, Sandra could see that. He loved her, and she had turned her back on him.

Katherine was an ungrateful wretch. How could she so easily spurn this world she had been born to? It wasn't fair for Katherine to have all this if she didn't appreciate it. Sandra would give anything to be able to trade places with her—anything at all.

The car zoomed uptown and came to a stop at the corner of Forty-fifth and Madison. The chauffeur stepped out and opened the door for her. Still slightly dazed, Sandra got out of the car and thanked him.

As the limousine sped away she stared longingly after it until it disappeared around the corner, taking away with it something special and magic. Something that should belong to her. It wasn't fair. It just wasn't fair.

## CHAPTER EIGHT

By the time Sandra got back to the office, it was close to three o'clock. Mrs. Morgan was furious, but Sandra didn't care. Something had happened to her today, something that gave her a feeling of command and importance and showed her her place in life. She was not about to let herself be intimidated by a drone like Mrs. Morgan.

She listened calmly while her supervisor launched into a tirade about responsibility and overstepping one's bounds. When Mrs. Morgan seemed to have said all she was going to say, Sandra looked at her placidly. "Are you trying to tell me I'm fired?"

"Why, I—no, of course not," Mrs. Morgan said, flustered.

"All right, then I'll get back to work." She turned on her heel, leaving the other woman with her mouth gaping.

Sandra was very pleased with herself. That old biddy had it coming. She didn't know where she got the courage to do that—she had wanted to do it for a long time, and now, today, she could. After today she could do anything.

The library was a mess. The girl who had taken

over for her didn't know where anything belonged, and books, magazines and files were strewn about the shelves haphazardly. Sandra was annoyed. The library was her private domain, and she didn't like anybody interfering with her sense of order. When she had come to work there, she had found it in a shambles, and she prided herself on the fact that she had turned it into a truly useful research library. The staff had been amazed by what she had done, and even Charles Roth himself had come down to see her handiwork. He had given her a raise on the spot.

She spent what was left of the afternoon putting everything just right. She didn't mind, because she had to know exactly where everything was. Then when people came in she could put her finger on what they needed almost before the words were out of their mouths. And they depended on her to do just that. It was after five when she locked up.

Katherine was waiting at the reception desk when Sandra emerged from her sanctuary.

"Hi," she said. "I haven't seen you all day. How'd it go at the doctor's?"

"I'll tell you about it later," Sandra said curtly, glancing at the crowd of co-workers waiting for the elevator. She didn't especially want anyone listening in to the story of medical problems that she intended to tell Katherine.

Sandra stepped into the elevator ahead of Katherine. She was shoved to the back. Standing behind her as the car descended, Sandra appraised

Katherine's hair. She didn't like the way it was looking.

When they got down to the lobby and Katherine turned to wait for her, Sandra said, "When was the last time you had your hair cut?"

Katherine tugged at a lock of hair hanging over one eye. "I don't know. Do you think I need it?"

"You certainly do. It's too long—it doesn't have any shape anymore."

Katherine looked slightly hurt. "I guess I've just forgotten about stuff like that in the past few weeks."

"Then call up and make an appointment—tomorrow."

"All right," Katherine said meekly.

They walked a few steps in silence, and then Sandra said, "I wish you hadn't asked me about the doctor in front of all those people. I don't want the whole world knowing my business."

Katherine slowed her pace. "I guess I can't do anything right today, can I?" she said bitterly.

Sandra looked back at her. "Don't be so sensitive, Katherine," she said, grabbing her arm and pulling her along. "Now, hurry up, or we'll miss the bus."

The next morning Sandra was at her desk busily clipping a copy of a week-old *Times* when the phone rang. It was the receptionist calling her out to the front desk to pick up a delivery. Thinking it was a package of books she was expecting, Sandra said she'd be out in a little while and went back to her clipping.

Five minutes later the phone rang again. It was the receptionist. "Sandra," she said, "you'd better get out here before someone else walks off with your delivery."

"Oh, all right," Sandra said. "I'm coming."

Wondering what all the bother was about, she got up and went to the front desk.

The receptionist gave her a wry smile. "Is it your birthday?" she asked.

"No. Why?"

"Those are for you." The girl pointed to a long white box. "Who are they from?"

"How should I know?" Sandra said, masking her surprise. "Probably some book salesman."

"Oh," the receptionist said, disappointed. "Too bad."

Sandra took her mysterious package back to the library. As a precaution she shut the door. Carefully unfolding the green tissue, she exulted in the perfume of twelve long-stemmed, perfectly formed yellow roses. There was an envelope attached, and when she took out the card she sank into her chair. It read: "Thank you for your kindness and the pleasure of your company, Philip Fielding."

Her hand was shaking, so she laid the card on the desk. Her eyes caressed each stroke of the strong, masculine handwriting. She was sure he had written it himself. He would not have entrusted Mrs. Porter to send the flowers for him. She would have been too curious about why Philip Fielding was sending roses to his daughter's best friend.

The giddy feeling of yesterday welled up in her again. Did the flowers mean that he had been attracted to her, too? Or was she reading more into it than was there?

Struggling to recover her composure, she took the card and slipped it into an inner pocket of her purse, where Katherine couldn't find it, then set the flowers to one side on her desk and opened the door. If anyone asked her where the roses came from, she would make up a story.

Half an hour later, the phone rang. "Library," she answered.

"Miss Jurgenson, this is Philip Fielding."

Sandra's heart started thumping. "Oh, hello," she responded, careful not to say his name because there was someone else in the library. "I got the roses. They're beautiful."

"I'm glad you like them," he said. "They're just a small gesture of my appreciation."

"But you didn't have to do that," Sandra said, trying to keep her tone casual, both for him and the ears she was sure were listening to her conversation.

"But I wanted to," he protested. "I just hope that they're not, well, awkward for you. If Katherine sees them, I think you'd better tell her they're from a boyfriend. I'm sure you have plenty of those."

"A few, yes. And that's what I planned to tell her."

"I thought you would know how to handle it." He hesitated. "How is Katherine? Still the same?"

"I'm afraid so."

"I see," he said thoughtfully. Then his voice resumed a cheerful tone. "Well, I'd better not keep you on the phone. Will I be hearing from you soon?"

"Yes, probably in another couple of days."

"Fine. I'll look forward to that. Good-bye."

"Good-bye." Sandra hung up the phone.

She was not imagining things. He really was attracted to her. But things would have to move slowly. They were both in a difficult position. He had his wife to think about, and she had Katherine.

Katherine zeroed in on the flowers the moment she stepped into the library. "Who sent you those?"

Sandra gave her a Mona Lisa smile.

"Oh, I get the picture—Stan the Man."

"Mmm, could be," Sandra said, but her eyes told Katherine that she had guessed right.

"He's really getting desperate, isn't he? When are you going to give the poor man a break and go out with him, Sandra?"

"Go out with him?" Sandra said with mock scorn. "Never!"

"Then you'd better stop leading him on." Katherine's tone had turned more serious.

"Why should I? It's just a game—he knows that."

"Oh, no he doesn't." Katherine pointed to the roses. "He thinks you mean it."

Sandra pouted. "Since when did *you* become his defender?"

A trace of red tinged Katherine's cheeks. "Well, I've gotten to know him better lately. He's been pretty nice to me, and I don't think he's such a bad guy. He deserves better treatment than that."

"Katherine!" Sandra said gleefully. "You've got the hots for him yourself!"

Katherine glared at her. "I have work to do." She turned and strode over to the files. When she found the folder she wanted, she pulled it out, noted it down on a clipboard, and went sailing past Sandra's desk.

"Katherine!" Sandra said, laughing.

Katherine halted. "What?"

"Did you sign that folder out?" Sandra asked.

"Of course," Katherine said in a clipped voice.

"Okay," Sandra said, grinning broadly. "I'll see you later then."

Katherine flashed her a look full of disdain and then walked out the door.

Sandra wondered if she had hit on a truth: Could Katherine really be attracted to Stan? It was possible. After all, he wasn't bad-looking, and she knew that he had been paying a lot of attention to Katherine. And in Katherine's vulnerable state it wouldn't be hard for anybody who was reasonably sympathetic to get to her.

And what about Stan? Could his interest be shifting from her to Katherine. That wasn't fair, he belonged to *her*—not that she really wanted him. But damn that Katherine! Everything always came so easily to her. Only this was one time when she wasn't going to get what she wanted. . . .

She was still brooding over this new situation when Stan himself walked in.

"Hi, gorgeous," he said, leaning over her desk. "I missed you yesterday. Where were you?"

"I was here," Sandra started to explain, but she saw the jealous look on Stan's face that meant he had spotted the flowers.

"Where'd those come from?" he asked, straightening up. "Your boyfriend?"

"Stan, you know you're my only boyfriend," Sandra said smoothly. "They're from a friend."

"Oh, yeah?" he said, looking meaningfully at her. "A *good* friend?"

"Not *that* good," Sandra smirked.

He gave her a half-hearted smile. "What kind of friend am I?"

"Oh, the best, Stan. The very best," she teased.

Stan's face fell. "Sandra," he said, "don't make fun of me. You've been putting me off for weeks now. When are you going to have dinner with me?"

"Oh, Stan, I'm sorry," Sandra gushed apologetically. "I wasn't making fun of you. Really, I wasn't. I don't know about dinner, though. Let's just have lunch for now, okay? See, I've never been involved with a married man before, and I guess it scares me."

"Yeah, I figured that was probably the problem," Stan said. "And I won't push you. When do you want to go to lunch?"

"Well, I guess tomorrow'd be fine."

"Okay. We'll go someplace nice."

"Sounds great."

Stan reached over and squeezed her hand. "See you tomorrow then."

He took her to a Japanese restaurant off Madison Avenue. The food was good, but Stan seemed to be in a hurry. The moment Sandra had finished eating, he called for the check.

"What's the rush?" Sandra asked.

Stan smiled at her mysteriously. "I've got something I want to show you."

"What is it?"

Stan shook his head. "You'll see." He took the check from the waitress, glanced at it, and threw some bills on the table. "Let's go," he said, pushing back his chair.

Sandra started to protest, but Stan was already helping her out of her chair.

He retrieved their coats from the checkroom, helped Sandra on with hers, and rushed her out onto the sidewalk.

"Stan, come on," Sandra said, irritated now. "Where are we going?"

"It's a surprise." His arm was around her waist, guiding her along the sidewalk toward Madison.

"I don't like surprises," Sandra said, sulking.

Stan pulled her closer to him. "You'll like this one." Then he let go of her as he hailed a cab over to the curb. "Seventy-fourth and Madison," he barked, hustling her inside.

"What's there?" Sandra asked.

"The surprise," Stan said, and took her hand in his.

Sandra gave him an exasperated look. "Okay, I give up," she said. "But this better not take too long. You know I'm not like you executives—I only get an hour for lunch."

"Don't worry." Stan patted her hand. "I'll have you back in plenty of time."

"You'd better. Or you can explain to Old Hatchet Face why I was late."

"Old Hatchet Face?"

"Mrs. Morgan."

Stan laughed. "Who, Ethel? I can take care of her. I've had her eating out of my hand for years."

"Then why don't you put in a good word for me with her? She gives me a pain in the ass."

"Forget about her, sweetheart. She doesn't count. Not with me on your side—and Charles."

Sandra stared at him. "Charles? He barely knows who I am," she scoffed.

"Not true. Old Charley thinks you've done a terrific job with the library, and"—he leaned toward her—"he thinks you're sexy."

"He does, huh?"

"Yeah, but don't get any ideas. He's already supporting two ex-wives and God knows how many girlfriends."

"He's not my type," Sandra said. "Too short."

The cab came to a stop as they reached their destination. Stan paid the driver and they got out. "This way," he said, and steered her several yards down Seventy-fourth Street to a renovated brownstone. Stan opened the front door. "Come on in," he said to Sandra, who was still standing on the sidewalk.

"Is this the surprise?" Sandra asked as she walked through the door.

"Not yet," Stan said. "It's inside." He unlocked the inner door, crossed a small lobby and unlocked a second door. "This is it," he said as he ushered Sandra inside.

It was a big apartment. The living room was

furnished with all the essentials, yet seemed somehow bare, almost like a hotel room. It was dark
and very quiet.

Sandra looked around as Stan turned on some
lights. "Is this yours?" she asked.

"No," Stan answered. "The building belongs to
a friend of mine. He only stays here occasionally
and he lets me use it anytime I want." He started
to take Sandra's coat, but she pulled away from
him.

"So is this your little love nest?" she asked sarcastically.

Stan walked over to her and put his hands on
her shoulders. "I brought you here because you
said you were afraid of getting involved with a
married man. I wanted you to see how it would
be with me. I'd never make you sneak around to
any crummy hotels—"

"Stan, that's not the point," Sandra said, taking
his hands off her shoulders. "Getting involved with
a married man always means sneaking around,
whether it's here or someplace else."

Stan threw up his hands. "All right, okay. I
know I said I wouldn't push you, but—"

"But what?"

"I just can't figure you out," he said gruffly.
"You lead me on like crazy, and now you've got
cold feet—because I'm married. You knew that
in the beginning. Why didn't you tell me to bug
off then?"

"Would it have done any good?"

"Hell, I don't know," he admitted. "Probably
not."

"Anyway, I didn't say I wouldn't get involved with you—but we have to be careful."

Stan looked at her. "Is that all?"

Sandra smiled. "Yes. So sit down and relax and let me take a look around this place."

"Here, let me show you," Stan said. He started toward a hallway off the living room but Sandra grabbed his arm.

"No," she said. "You sit down. I'd rather see for myself."

Stan did as she said, and Sandra walked out of the living room and down the hall. There was one bedroom and a bathroom next door. As she gazed around the sparsely furnished room, something clicked in her memory. There was an idea half forming in the back of her mind, but she pushed it away, refusing to let it take shape, and hurried back to the living room.

"This is a nice apartment," she said to Stan. "Too bad your friend hasn't done more with the decorating."

Stan shrugged. "I guess it suits his needs."

"And yours," Sandra said with a grin. "What about your needs? Does it suit them?"

"I guess it'll have to do."

Stan extended his hand to her. "Come here," he said. When she took his hand he pulled her onto his lap and kissed her roughly.

"Stan," Sandra gasped, struggling away from the pressure of his lips. "We can't do this now. I've got to get back to work."

"Forget about work," he said, trying to pull her face down to his again.

"I can't!" Sandra jerked her head away. "This isn't right, anyway. Let's come here sometime after work—when I won't feel so rushed."

"When? Tonight?"

"Not tonight, silly," Sandra laughed. "It's Friday. You've got to get home to your wife and kids."

"I'll take a later train."

Sandra shook her head. "No, tonight's no good. How about Monday night? Is that soon enough?"

"I guess it'll have to be," Stan groaned. "But I'll spend the whole weekend thinking about it."

Sandra nuzzled his ear. "You do that," she breathed. "Then you'll really be up for it."

Stan grabbed her face in his hands. "You bitch!" He covered her mouth with his.

She was only a little late, and nobody seemed to have noticed—not even Mrs. Morgan. Sandra took off her coat, sat down at her desk, and put her head in her hands. What was she thinking of? She had never meant for anything like this to happen with Stan. She was only moderately attracted to him, and now she had all but gone to bed with him. What had gotten into her? Why did she keep doing these crazy things? It was that way when she had gone to see Katherine's father, and now she had done it again today with Stan. Could she be losing her mind? Maybe she was racked with guilt over Ted Hanley's murder and she was trying to make it up to all the other men in the world. Could that possibly be it? Or was it something else? Something so sinister that she couldn't even admit it to herself.

Friday night. Along First Avenue the bars were beginning to fill. Ziggy's was bustling. But Katherine and Sandra had not been out since that fatal night with Ted Hanley. Neither of them had the heart for it anymore. Katherine had no heart for anything anymore. Night after night she picked listlessly at her dinner, then retreated to her room, leaving Sandra to stare at the television set and wonder, sorrow and outrage mingling, what had happened to their lives.

Tonight she had prevailed upon Katherine to have dinner out, though Katherine had shown little enthusiasm. Sandra pressed her. They had even talked about seeing a movie later. Sandra was looking forward to it. It would be the first time in weeks that they had done anything normal. She had managed to push all her anxious thoughts of the afternoon out of her mind, and she was feeling almost carefree.

But Katherine was sullen. She had talked little since they had met at the end of the day, and during dinner the conversation was mostly one-sided, with Sandra making comments and asking questions and getting nothing but monosyllabic responses from Katherine.

Finally Sandra put down her fork. "What the hell is wrong with you tonight?" she asked Katherine angrily. "You haven't said two decent words to me since we left the office."

"I just don't feel like talking," Katherine said morosely.

"Why? Did something happen today?"

Katherine shot her a look of venom. "I don't know. *You* tell me."

"And what is that supposed to mean?"

"You know damn well what I'm talking about!" Katherine's voice was shrill, and several diners turned their heads to stare.

"Katherine, lower your voice," Sandra hissed. "You're making a spectacle of yourself."

"As if I cared," Katherine said, her voice rising. "They can all go fuck themselves!"

Sandra stiffened visibly, and then turned around to search for their waiter. When she caught his eye she signaled him over to the table.

"What are you doing?" Katherine asked.

"Getting the check. We're leaving."

"But I don't want—"

"I don't care what you want!" Sandra burst out. "I'm not going to sit here and let you make a fool of me!"

Katherine's lower lip trembled. Her anger now dissipated, she was fighting to hold back the tears.

Sandra stared at her in disbelief. The change in Katherine had been so mercurial that she did not know how to react. She decided that the best course of action would be to get Katherine out of the restaurant as quickly and as inconspicuously as she could.

When the waiter brought the check she paid him immediately and then hustled Katherine into her coat and out the door.

"I don't feel like going to a movie anymore," Katherine mumbled.

"I didn't think so. Let's go home."

"I feel like walking."

"All right. We'll walk home."

They covered a few blocks in silence before Katherine suddenly turned to Sandra. "Where did you go today?" she asked.

"What, you mean at lunchtime?"

Katherine nodded.

"I told you. I had lunch with a friend."

"What friend?"

"Nobody you know."

"It was Stan, wasn't it?"

Sandra caught her breath. "What makes you think that?" she said, trying to sound casual.

"Because I know you."

Sandra didn't answer. She kept her eyes fixed straight ahead.

"Come on," Katherine badgered. "Tell me the truth. It was Stan, wasn't it?"

"Yes!" Sandra shouted defiantly. "Yes, I had lunch with Stan today. Why shouldn't I? Weren't you the one who said I should stop leading him on?"

"Then why did you lie to me about it?" Katherine asked softly.

"I didn't lie to you! I just didn't tell you who I was having lunch with. Do I have to account to you for every minute?"

"No, but you make *me*."

"Katherine, I do not! If I make you tell me where you're going and who you're seeing it's only because I'm concerned about you. You know you haven't been yourself lately."

"I know, and I don't mind that, Sandra. Honestly, I don't. But you were gone for lunch on

Wednesday and then again today and I—" Katherine's voice diminished to a whisper, "I don't like it when you go away and leave me." She burst into tears.

Sandra stopped walking and put her arm around Katherine. She wanted to tell Katherine how she felt. She wanted to say: "I won't leave you, Katherine. I'll never leave you." But she did not dare say the words.

## CHAPTER NINE

Katherine's chest rose and fell regularly, and Sandra watched her for a moment before she tiptoed across her bedroom to the dresser. Ever so carefully she opened a drawer and pulled out Katherine's best sweater. It was a beauty—baby-blue cashmere with a cowlneck. Sandra put it on over her slacks and admired herself in the mirror. The fact that the sweater was rather snug only showed off her breasts to greater advantage. Next, she fumbled among Katherine's jewelry and picked out a pair of silver earrings and a shiny cuff bracelet. For added measure, she dabbed some of Katherine's Joy behind her ears. Then she went to the hall closet and put on Katherine's coat. As she slipped out of the apartment, closing the door soundlessly behind her, she felt a surge of reckless excitement. After all, she deserved some fun. And Katherine need never know.

She was still smiling to herself as she stepped into the bar. It felt so good to be out among people again, out where there was music and laughter and something to do besides playing nursemaid for Katherine.

It was a typical, noisy Friday night crowd, and

as Sandra made her way through the crush of bodies she grinned flirtatiously at several men who tried to get her attention. But they didn't interest her; tonight she could afford to be choosy. She wasn't about to waste herself on any smarmy junior execs; no, tonight she wanted to meet someone exciting, different, a challenge.

"Hey, beautiful," a male voice behind her said. "Can I buy you a drink?"

Sandra turned around slowly. He was tall and not bad-looking. He wasn't what she was after, but he'd do for now.

"Sure, why not?"

"What'll it be?" he asked, looking her up and down and obviously approving of what he saw.

"Gin and tonic."

He got her the drink. "By the way," he said, "my name's Dave. What's yours?"

Sandra gave him an inscrutable smile. "I'd rather not say."

"So, you're a mystery lady?"

"For tonight."

"Well, I hate to disappoint you, but you're not the only mystery around here tonight." His eyes gleamed mischievously.

"Where's my rival?" Sandra asked, with a mock pout.

"See that guy over in the corner?" he said, pointing to a man in a dark overcoat. "He's a cop. He's working on a *real* mystery."

At the word "cop," Sandra felt a quiver of excitement go down her spine. "What mystery is that?" she asked coolly.

"Remember the guy who was killed a few weeks ago on Seventy-seventh Street?"

"Not really," Sandra said vaguely. "What about him?"

"Well, he used to hang out in the singles' bars. So all these cops have been going to places on the East Side, showing people his picture and asking them if they've ever seen him around. I even talked to them myself a couple of times."

"Oh, wow," Sandra said. "What did they ask you?"

"Not much. They just showed me this guy's picture and asked me if I recognized him. I didn't, so that was about it."

"What are they, detectives?" Sandra asked.

"Sure. Homicide, I guess."

"I've never talked to a detective before. It must be exciting."

"Nah. They're pretty dull, if you ask me."

"I think I'm going over there," Sandra said suddenly. "Maybe he'll ask me some questions."

"Hey, wait a minute," Dave shouted after her. But Sandra was already gone, pushing her way through the crowd.

Her heart pounding, she sidled up to the man in the dark overcoat. He had black, curly hair and heavy features, and in the dim light she couldn't tell how old he was. Maybe forty.

"Hi," she said as he looked up at her. "Are you a detective?"

He grinned. "Does it show that much?"

She shook her head. "Actually, someone pointed you out to me."

"Oh, yeah?" he said, eying her. "What'd they say?"

"They said you were asking questions about some guy who used to come in here who was murdered."

"Yeah, that's right. I did talk to a few people. Only I'm not really working now. I'm off-duty."

"Oh," Sandra said, sounding disappointed. "I thought maybe I might know this guy. I used to come in here all the time, but I haven't been around in a few weeks."

"Well, just a minute," he said, reaching into his pocket. "Let me show you his picture." He brought out a photo of Ted Hanley.

Sandra stared at it thoughtfully, pursing her lips. "Mmm, I don't think so," she said, amazing even herself with how convincing she seemed. "He looks sort of familiar, but I don't know. After a while they all look the same to me. What happened to him, anyway?"

"He was stabbed." He put the photo away. "In his apartment, up on Seventy-seventh Street. Didn't you read about it?"

"I don't read the papers anymore. They upset me."

"Then I don't think you want to hear about this guy, do you?"

She shook her head. "No, I guess not. You're probably not supposed to talk about it, anyway. But I'm fascinated by your work."

"Is that so?" he said, sipping his drink. "Just what about it fascinates you?"

"Oh, you know. Tracking down murderers, that sort of thing."

"It's not like TV," he said. "Would you believe I never shot anyone? In fact, I hardly ever take my gun out of the holster."

"Then what's it like?" Sandra asked breathlessly.

"Here," he said, getting up, "why don't you sit down and let me buy you a refill. And then I'll tell you all about it."

Sandra smiled at him as she sat down on the stool. "I'm drinking gin and tonic," she said. He ordered her another.

"What do you do when you don't have any clues?" she asked him after the fresh drink arrived. "Where do you start then?"

"Mostly, you look for witnesses," he said. "Somebody who might have been at the scene or who saw the victim with somebody."

"But don't those people usually come forward?" Sandra asked innocently.

"Are you kidding?" He laughed. "Why do you think I have to go around busting my ass, knocking on doors, asking the same questions all the time?"

"But what if you don't find anybody who saw anything?"

"We keep on trying—until it doesn't look like we're getting anywhere."

"Then what do you do?"

He shrugged. "We give up."

"You just forget about it?" Sandra prodded.

"Sometimes we get a new lead," he said indifferently. Then he looked at her. "How come a pretty girl like you is so interested in all this?"

Sandra felt all the blood drain out of her face.

She prayed he didn't notice. "Just curious," she said, trying to sound offhand. Time to change the subject, she thought desperately. "So what brings you in here tonight?" she asked.

"Same thing as you." He leaned toward her.

She laughed. "What do you think I'm here for?"

"A good time," he said, draping his arm around the back of the stool. "Maybe have a few laughs, meet people."

"Well, I met *you*, didn't I?" Sandra said coyly. So he wasn't all that attractive, but she was living dangerously just talking to him. And that made him far more exciting to her tonight than any sexy stud.

He smiled knowingly at her and leaned closer. As he moved forward his coat and sport jacket opened wide, and Sandra caught a glimpse of the black shape of his revolver. It sent delicious shivers through her whole body.

"Don't look now," she said in a low, seductive voice, "but your gun is showing."

"It doesn't scare you, does it?" he asked, his tone imitating hers.

"Uh-uh. I think it's kind of sexy." Her eyes, fixed on his, were openly inviting.

He straightened up and set his drink down on the bar. "What d'you say we leave this place?" he asked. "Go somewhere quiet so we can talk. You can tell me all about yourself."

"That's fine with me." Sandra got up, smiling at him. "What place did you have in mind?"

He tossed some money on the bar. "Oh, we'll think of something."

He steered her through the crowd, and as he

was opening the door for her, he stopped. "Hey, I don't even know your name," he said. "What is it?"

She looked up at him and hesitated just a moment before she laughed and said softly, "It's Katherine. Katherine Fielding."

## CHAPTER TEN

Sandra sipped her drink nervously. Stan's hand was on her leg under the table, and she wished he would take it away. Having dinner with Stan before they went to his little hideaway had been her idea, but now she wasn't so sure it had been a good one—he was getting drunk.

When he picked her up after work she suspected that he had already been to a bar downstairs, to fortify himself for the evening. Now he was on his second drink in the restaurant, and it was becoming all too obvious to her that Stan couldn't hold his liquor. She thought of the big, burly detective she had spent Friday night with, and it made Stan seem all the more pathetic.

"Stan," she said, taking his hand off her leg, "don't you think we should order dinner now?"

"Sure, honey," he nodded heavily, "anything you say."

The waiter appeared, as if on cue, and presented them with menus.

Sandra bitchily ordered the most expensive item on the menu. If Stan was going to humiliate her like this, then he would have to pay for it.

He ordered a bottle of wine to go with dinner,

and Sandra groaned inwardly. She had visions of herself with a drunken Stan propped up against her, trying to get him out of the restaurant.

The first course arrived, and it was excellent. Sandra thought to herself that the meal would probably be her only pleasure in an evening that was otherwise going to be horrendous. He was concentrating on his soup. Sandra looked away. Then she became aware that he had lowered his spoon and was intent on her now, considering something. Then it came. "Say," he said carefully, "where's your girlfriend tonight?"

"She's home. Why?"

A flicker of amusement crossed Stan's face. "Is she alone?"

"I suppose so. I don't know, I'm not her social secretary."

Stan laughed—too heartily—and Sandra squirmed in her seat and averted her eyes from him.

"Hey," he said, pawing at her arm. When Sandra turned to look at him, he leaned closer. "Tell me about her," he said. "Does she like men?"

"Of course she does," Sandra said, removing his hand from her arm.

He smiled knowingly. "I'll bet she's frigid."

Sandra pulled away from him. She started to tell Stan that it was none of his business, but a sudden perverse impulse stopped her. "No," she said boldly, "she's not. And I ought to know."

Stan's eyes widened and his mouth dropped open. Sandra just sat there, looking steadily at him, and loving every minute of his reaction.

"You mean, you two—" he managed to say finally.

"Mmm, not exactly," Sandra teased. "There was a man with us at the time."

"A threesome?" Stan asked, his eyes suddenly glowing with interest.

"That's what they call it. Why, does that turn you on?"

Stan leered at her. "I'll say!"

"Haven't you ever done it?"

"Nah, I never got the chance before."

Sandra looked at him sharply. "What do you mean 'before'?"

Stan moved in closer. "Well, I thought maybe you'd call your friend up and get her to come over to the place tonight. We could have a lot of fun."

"Nothing doing," Sandra said, pushing him away. "Katherine would never go for it."

"Aw, why not?" Stan wheedled. "She likes me, I know she does. Why don't you jus' give it a try? I'll bet she says okay."

"I'll think about it," Sandra said. She looked up to see the waiter about to serve the main course. "Let's just enjoy our food now," she said, "and we'll talk about it later. All right?"

Stan agreed, unwillingly, and they settled down to eating. He even seemed to be sobering up a little—until he polished off more than half the bottle of wine with the meal. Then he started coaxing Sandra again.

"Come on, come on," he kept saying. "Call 'er up."

Sandra ignored him and went on eating. Finally

she said, "Stan, forget this crazy idea. Katherine won't do it. I know her."

"Aw, come on," he begged. "Give it a try." He fished in his pocket for some change. "Here's a dime. Go call her." He pressed the coin into Sandra's hand. She was struck by how clammy his fingers were.

"Oh, all right," she said, throwing her napkin on the table and standing. "I'll do it."

She headed for the ladies' room. There was a pay telephone just outside its door. She had no intention of calling Katherine. She would simply use the ladies' room, and when she got back to the table she'd tell Stan that Katherine had refused to come.

She hesitated as she passed the phone. *Would* Katherine come if she asked her to? Funny thing is, she might. And why shouldn't she? Sandra thought that she could probably use some help in handling the drunken Stan, anyway, and after all she had done for Katherine. . . .

She picked up the phone, deposited the dime, and dialed her own number. After five rings Katherine's voice said thickly, "Hello?"

Great, Sandra thought, she sounds drugged. "Hi," she said brightly. "It's Sandra."

"Where are you?"

"You know. I'm out with Stan."

"Oh, yeah." There was a pause, then snidely, "How's your date?"

"Horrible, really awful. He's drunk."

"What a shame."

"Katherine, stop trying to be cute. I need your help."

"What for?"

"He's a mess, and I can't handle him by myself."

"What do you want me to do?"

"I want you to come over here and help me sober him up. Then maybe we can get him on a train or put him in a hotel."

"Where's 'here'?"

"It's an apartment at Seventy-fourth and Madison."

"Why can't he just stay there?"

"Because it's not his apartment. I've got to get him out of here, and I can't do it alone. Please, Katherine. You've got to do it. There's nobody else I can ask."

"Oh, Christ, Sandra. I'm not even dressed."

"Then get dressed and take a cab over here. The address is—"

"Just a minute. Wait'll I get a pencil." A pause. "Okay, what is it?"

"Twenty-seven East Seventy-fourth Street, apartment one. It's right off Madison—toward Park."

"Okay, I'll be there. But it's going to take me a little while."

"You're a doll."

"Sure." Katherine hung up.

Sandra figured it would take Katherine at least twenty minutes to get there. The restaurant was about ten blocks from the apartment, if Stan paid the check right away and they got a cab immediately, they could be there in ten minutes. Suddenly she felt feverish. Why was she doing

all this? Thank God, she didn't have time to think
about it.

She walked back to the table and said as calmly as she could, "Okay, Stan. I talked her into it.
She's coming, so we have to leave right away."

Stan's eyes shone. "No kiddin'! That's great—
that's fantastic. This is goin' to be *some* evening."

Stan fumbled with the key as he tried to fit it
into the lock of the apartment door. "Goddamn
key," he muttered to himself as he tried again.

Sandra was standing behind him, listening for
the outer door. What would happen if Katherine
arrived before they even got into the apartment?
She checked her watch. It had been fifteen minutes since she called. This was cutting it too close.
"Do you want me to try?" she asked Stan.

"Nah, I got it now," he said, and the door clicked
open. "Come on in, honey." He was inside, grop-
ing for the light switch.

"It's right behind you," Sandra said, and pointed
to a switch she could see in the light from the
lobby.

Stan hit the switch and the lights came on.
"That's better." He shut the door. "Here, gimme
your coat." Stan took their coats and dumped them
on a chair. "Wanna drink?"

"Not now. Let's just sit down and wait for
Katherine. You look a little unsteady on your
feet."

"Me?" Stan laughed. He was swaying slightly.
"I'm fine. Jus' fine." He lunged at Sandra. "Let's
not wait for Katherine."

Sandra stepped aside and he fell against a

table, knocking an ashtray to the floor, where it shattered with a loud report. Sandra jumped, startled by the noise. She put her hand to her chest and felt the too rapid beating of her heart. "Stan!" she said in a high-pitched voice, "sit down before you break something else!"

Looking sheepish, Stan collapsed into a chair. "Sorry," he said, "guess maybe I am a little drunk."

Sandra sat down in a chair facing him and closed her eyes. But instead of blackness, she saw Ted Hanley. He was laughing, coming toward her, brandishing the belt. She opened her eyes to make the image go away and saw Stan, staring at her.

"Hey, don' fall asleep on me," he said.

Sandra looked at him for a long moment and then turned away. "No, I won't," she sighed.

A buzzer sounded, and Sandra jumped again.

"Boy, you're nervous," Stan laughed. " 'S only the door buzzer." He struggled out of the chair and went to answer it.

Sandra was trembling. What was she going to do now?

Stan pressed the buzzer to unlock the inner door to the building, flung open the apartment door, and called out to Katherine, "Hiya, beautiful! Come on in!"

Sandra heard Katherine's footsteps crossing the lobby and her mumbled response to Stan. When she walked through the door he grabbed her in a bear hug. "What are you doing, Stan?" she said, trying futilely to disentangle herself from his embrace. As she twisted her head away from him, her eyes fell on Sandra, and stared daggers at her.

Finally Stan let her go and he shut the door

behind them. "Well, here we are," he said, rubbing his hands together. "Jus' the three of us."

Katherine gave Sandra a puzzled look. Her eloquent shrug answered Katherine's unasked question.

"Take off your coat and stay awhile," Stan said, tugging at Katherine's sleeve.

"No, I think I'll keep it on," Katherine said, and stepped away from Stan's grasp.

"Aw, come on," Stan whined.

"You'd better take it off," Sandra said to her. "As you can see, this is going to take some doing." Her eyes indicated Stan.

"Oh, all right," Katherine sighed. She took off her coat and put it on top of Stan's and Sandra's. She was dressed in a sweater and jeans.

"Now, that's better," Stan said, his eyes wandering over her body.

Looking uncomfortable, Katherine folded her arms across her chest and sat down.

Stan plopped himself down on the arm of her chair and leaned heavily toward her. "Whatsa matter with you, Kathy?" he asked. "Don' you wanta have a good time?"

Recoiling from the alcohol fumes on his breath, Katherine snapped, "Don't call me that!" and rudely shoved him away.

"Oh, pardon me, your royal highness," Stan said, teetering on his feet. He attempted to make a sweeping bow, but when he leaned forward he was thrown off balance completely and he pitched forward onto the floor. Sandra sprang up and tried to catch him, but his weight was too much for her.

"Stan! Get up," she said through clenched teeth. "You're disgusting." He looked blankly up at her and then erupted into raucous giggles.

Sandra threw him a look of contempt and walked over to where Katherine was sitting. "See what I mean?" she said in a low voice so Stan could not hear. "He's impossible. What are we going to do with him?"

"Why don't we give him some coffee?"

"No, I tried that before," Sandra lied. "He won't drink it."

"Maybe he will now."

"No, I have another idea. Why don't we take him into the bedroom and let him sleep for a while? Maybe that'll sober him up."

Katherine looked doubtful. "If he goes to sleep, it'll be hard to wake him up."

"Well, it's the only thing I can think of," Sandra said testily. "If we can't wake him up, I guess we'll just have to leave him here."

"What about the people who live here?"

"I don't know who they are. When they come home, they'll just have to take care of him."

"Okay, now how do we get him into the bedroom?"

Sandra glanced at Stan, who was still rolling on the floor, laughing to himself. "I guess you take one arm and I take the other," she said.

Katherine got up and they went to Stan and stood over him. "Stan, get up," Sandra said. "We're taking you into the bedroom."

Stan looked up at them and grinned. "Hey, I'm seeing double," he chuckled. "There are two beautiful women begging me to go into the bedroom with them." He covered his eyes with his hands and then quickly took them away. "Oh, they're still there," he said, giggling.

Sandra reached down and grabbed one arm. Katherine took hold of the other. "Come on, Stan," Sandra said as they pulled him up. "That's right." She had coaxed him to a sitting position. "Now stand up. We'll help you." They pulled on his arms and he lurched to his feet. "Put your arms around us for support," she ordered. "Now walk." Stan obeyed her, and they maneuvered him across the living room, down the hallway, and into the bedroom, where he fell heavily onto the bed.

"Okay, girls, come on. I'm ready," he said, and held out his arms to them.

"Right, Stan. That's very funny," Sandra said quickly before Katherine could realize he was serious. "Before you take us both on though, I think you should have a little rest."

"Well, maybe," Stan said. "But jus' a little one."

"Okay, fine," Sandra said soothingly. "We'll be back in a few minutes."

"I won' go anywhere."

"Good," Sandra said, and propelled Katherine back to the living room.

"Whew!" Katherine exhaled, sitting down. "How did you manage to get yourself in this mess?"

"Me? I didn't do anything. He had started before he even picked me up."

"I'm really surprised at him," Katherine mused. "I would have thought he could hold his liquor better than this." She grinned. "I bet he doesn't have the nerve to face us tomorrow. I'll have to make a special point of going into his office— just to see his reaction."

"Maybe he won't remember," Sandra said idly. She sat down, but then jumped up and began pacing around the living room.

Katherine watched her, curious. Then she saw the fragments of the glass ashtray on the floor and pointed to them. "Don't tell me he did that?" she said.

"Yes." Sandra ran her hand across her eyes. "He was getting rough with me and I had to push him off. That's when he fell and broke it."

Katherine's expression suddenly became concerned. "What did he do to you?"

"Oh, you know." Sandra waved her hand aimlessly in the air. "He kept slobbering on me, and when I tried to get away he grabbed me and he— well, he hit me a couple of times."

"He hit you?" Katherine asked, wide-eyed. "But he seems so harmless, just a silly drunk."

"I know. He fooled me, too—until I made him mad by fighting him off. Then he got vicious and started slapping me around. I'll probably be all black-and-blue tomorrow," Sandra said, rubbing her jaw. She knew she was giving another virtuoso performance like the one she'd given the cop Friday night. Katherine had no inkling about that. Well, what Katherine didn't know wouldn't hurt her. "Anyway," she went on, lowering her voice to a whisper, "I got really scared so I told him that I had to go to the bathroom and I went into the bedroom and called you."

"Oh, my God, I'm glad you did. Why didn't you tell me this before?"

"I—I was afraid you'd get excited and call the police or something."

"Well, maybe we should."

"No, we can't do that. He'd be furious. He'd do something to us—"

"So what! If he's dangerous we should let the police handle him."

"But, Katherine, we can't do that. We'd have to go down to the station house and file charges, and they'd probably ask us a lot of questions." Sandra looked at her meaningfully. "Do you see what I mean?"

"Oh." Katherine lowered her eyes. "No. You're right."

Just then there was a shout from the bedroom, and the two women exchanged glances. "Do you want me to go?" Katherine asked.

"No," Sandra said, shaking her head dejectedly. "No. That's all right. I'll go." She made her way from the living room to the bedroom.

Stan was completely naked, his clothes lying in a heap on the floor. "Hey, where's your frien'?" he asked. "I'm ready to go."

Sandra stared vacantly at him, his image swimming before her blurred eyes. She heard a roaring in her ears and stood frozen, suspended in a moment of time that was both present and past combined. She felt as though she were dying, as though she couldn't breathe. Because if she breathed, she would have to move; and if she moved, she could never dare look back. . . .

"Aw, come on," Stan was whining. "Go get her, willya?"

Wordlessly, Sandra turned back into the hall-way.

After a couple of steps she doubled over, clutching at her ribs, silently gasping for air. She closed her eyes and prayed for the strength to breathe, to go on living. And immediately Ted Hanley's image was there, vicious, sadistic, menacing. She started to choke—and then she suddenly felt the air coming in. Sweet air, going down her throat, into her lungs, saving her. She gulped at it and was instantly calmer. Now she could do what she had to do.

She continued into the living room. Katherine studied her face in dismay. "Sandra, what's wrong with you?" she asked. "You're as white as a sheet."

"Nothing," Sandra answered, avoiding her eyes. "I'm just getting T—*Stan* some aspirin." She picked up her purse.

Katherine did not notice the slip. "If he gives you any more trouble," she said, "just give me a yell. Okay?"

"Mmm hmm," Sandra murmured as she turned down the hall. Her heart was beating so wildly she could feel the blood throbbing in her temples.

She hesitated outside the door, steeling herself. Stan lifted his head from the pillow as she entered the room and started to say something to her, but Sandra put her finger to her lips, signaling him to be quiet.

"Stan, listen," she whispered, "I have an idea. It's kind of weird, but I think you might get off on it. It's a little game that Katherine likes to play."

"You mean somethin' kinky?" Stan asked in a stage whisper.

"Shh," Sandra responded. "We don't want her to hear you. That would spoil everything." She sat down on the bed next to him and he reached for her. "Wait a minute," she said, pushing his hand away. "I'll tell you what you have to do. First of all, I'll get halfway undressed—so it looks like you've been tearing my clothes off. And then you take your belt and start hitting me with it—not hard enough to hurt me. But I'll pretend that you are and I'll call out to Katherine. Then she'll come running in to 'rescue' me—and she'll take care of you herself."

"What's she gonna do to me?" Stan asked, a trace of wariness in his eyes.

"Oh, wow," Sandra forced a laugh. "What *won't* she do to you!"

Stan grinned. "Boy, she's a wild one, isn't she? You'd never know it to look at her."

"So what do you think?" Sandra pressed him. "Do you want to play this game?"

"What the hell. Sure." Stan's eyes gleamed. "But when will it be your turn?"

"Right after Katherine's finished with you—if you can take it," Sandra teased.

"You just wait," he growled.

"Okay, let's get started," Sandra said, getting up. "You get your belt out and I'll get ready." She took her purse and put it on top of the dresser, the only other piece of furniture in the room. Glancing over at Stan, who was preoccupied with extricating his belt from the loops of his pants, she opened her purse and dug in the bottom of it until she found what she was after. Her hand was shaking as her fingers curled around the cold silver of the letter opener. She had kept it in her purse ever since the day Katherine had given it to her, telling herself that she would get rid of it at the first opportunity. Funny how she had never gotten around to it. Now she slipped it out of her purse and positioned it on the dresser so that her purse blocked Stan's view of it. Not that he'd notice it anyway, but it would spoil the experiment if he did, and she wanted to take no chances.

That done, she unzipped the back of her dress part way and pulled it down over one shoulder, then pulled down her bra strap on the same side and ran her fingers through her hair, tousling it so that she would look as though Stan had been mauling her.

"I'm ready," she said to Stan, "are you?"

"Am I ever." His eyes were glued to her half-exposed breasts. Sandra could see by the size of his erection that he wasn't kidding.

"Okay," she said, getting on the bed. "Now you start hitting me and I'll scream for Katherine. Try to make it look good—like you're really beating me up. It's okay if you even hit me a little—but not too hard. And when Katherine comes running in, lay it on real thick."

Stan playfully lifted the belt and flopped it down on the bed.

"No!" Sandra whispered. "Not like that—harder. Make it look real!"

He whipped the belt back, and this time it

came down with a sharp snap. "That's better," Sandra said. "Keep it up and I'll start screaming."

There was a smile on his face as he brought the belt down again—a little harder. Then Sandra screamed, and her scream was so convincing that Stan almost stopped. But Sandra motioned to him to continue. He swung the belt again.

"Katherine!" There were hard, racing footsteps in the hall. "Katherine! Help me!"

Katherine ran into the room and came to a dead stop. Intent on his performance, Stan snapped the belt again. "Katherine! Stop him!" Sandra begged. At Sandra's cries Stan started to snicker, turning his face away so Katherine couldn't see it. But her attention was not on Stan. She was standing, gaping at Sandra, who was crouched on the bed writhing and crying as if she were in great pain.

"Katherine," Sandra gasped, "behind you—on the dresser—use it—stop him. *Please*, Katherine —help me!"

Uncertainly, Katherine turned toward the dresser. For a moment she stood paralyzed, staring stupidly at the letter opener. Then her hands flew to her eyes to block out the sight.

Stan was still swinging the belt, and Sandra wailed in anguish from the bed, "Katherine—use it! You've got to—stop him—before he *kills* me!"

Katherine pulled her hands away from her eyes, her face contorted in agony. Cautiously, she extended her right hand, inch by inch, to the letter opener. Then in one motion, she jerked it up, whirled, and slammed it into Stan's back.

He fell to his knees, wheezing and choking and

grabbing at his back. As he went down, Katherine pulled the blade out of his back. The wound was not very deep and only produced a trickle of blood. She dropped the letter opener to the floor and stood there, her eyes fixed on Stan. He had fallen to his hands and knees and was moaning loudly.

Carefully, Sandra got up from the bed, watching Katherine, waiting to see what she did next. But she did not move, so Sandra went and stood beside her, looking down at the wounded figure on the floor. She hesitated a moment, not knowing what to do, and then she took Katherine by the hand and led her into the bathroom. She sat her down, and was surprised to see that there was only a small smudge of blood on Katherine's hand and the sleeve of her sweater. She left her, shutting the door behind her. Slowly, she made her way to the spot where the letter opener gleamed on the bare floor. She picked it up, her mouth set in a grim line. Stan was still bent over, softly crying, "Help me, help me." Sandra raised the letter opener above her head and plunged it into his back. Again and again, until there was no more sound.

## CHAPTER ELEVEN

Sandra's heart sank as the cab pulled up in front of their building. She had seen the uniformed figure standing in the lobby and recognized at once that it was Freddie, the one doorman who knew them well and who loved to talk. *Damn it,* she thought to herself, *how am I going to get Katherine upstairs, past Freddie, without his noticing that she's behaving like a zombie?*

She paid the driver and helped Katherine out of the cab. When Freddie rushed out to open the door for them, she decided to take the bull by the horns. "Hi, Freddie," she said, guiding Katherine through the doors. "Do me a favor, will you, and go get the elevator for us? Katherine's feeling kind of sick and I want to get her right upstairs."

"Sure," Freddie said, glancing at Katherine. He raced across the lobby to the elevators and pressed the button, holding the door open for them while they slowly crossed the lobby.

"Thanks a lot," Sandra said, pushing Katherine ahead of her into the elevator. Katherine's face was pale and immobile, her eyes were fixed on the ground.

Freddie studied Katherine again and shook his head. "She sure doesn't look too good," he said.

"I know," Sandra sighed. "I've got to put her to bed right away. Good night, Freddie."

"Good night." He pushed the button and let the elevator door close.

Sandra turned to look at Katherine again as they ascended to the fourteenth floor. The expression on her face had not changed since the moment she dropped the letter opener; it did not change when Sandra took her hand and led her down the hall. As Sandra fitted her key in the lock, she remembered how Stan had fumbled with the lock to the apartment on Seventy-fourth Street. It seemed like years ago.

Katherine had left a light on when she went out, and a thought suddenly seized Sandra: Had Katherine known what she was rushing off to she never would have gone. But, of course, Katherine had no way of knowing. She herself had not known, not then. Or had she? She pushed the thought out of her mind—it was too disturbing.

Fatigue was settling into the very marrow of her bones. She was too tired to even think anymore. All she wanted to do was sleep, but first she had to take care of Katherine.

She took Katherine into her room and sat her down on the bed. "Katherine," she said, "can you get undressed?" No response. Katherine had not spoken a word since the scene with Stan. Sandra was puzzled; this was a different reaction than she had had after Ted Hanley's murder. Then she had cried, become hysterical. This time there was nothing, not even a sign that she knew where she was, or that Sandra was there, taking care of her.

After she'd taken off both their coats, Sandra pulled Katherine's sweater over her head, then bent down and tugged off her boots. She got Katherine to stand up again while she unzipped her jeans and pushed both her jeans and panties down so that they dropped around her ankles. Putting her arm around Katherine's waist for support, she helped her step out of them. She got out a nightgown, slipped it over Katherine's head, pulled back the covers, and put her into bed, while Katherine suffered the manipulations passively, with no more response than if she had been a mannequin. She lay on her back, her eyes wide open, staring at the ceiling.

Sandra looked at her, perplexed. She couldn't just leave her like this; she'd better give her something to knock her out. So she turned and went into the bathroom, got out two of Katherine's sleeping pills and a glass of water, and brought them back to the bedroom. She pressed the pills into Katherine's hand and lifted her head and shoulders until she was sitting up. She thought she glimpsed a slight reaction to the sleeping pills in Katherine's eyes; anyway, she seemed to be looking at them. But she still did not move, so Sandra took the two capsules out of Katherine's hand, pulled down her jaw and thrust the pills into her mouth. "Swallow," she ordered, putting the glass of water to her lips. Katherine took the water and the pills and then coughed, but even that did not wake her from her state of shock. So

Sandra put her head back down on the pillow, turned off the lights, and shut the door behind her.

She dragged herself into her own room, tore off her clothes and fell into bed. Just before she drifted off to sleep, she remembered that she had to go to work tomorrow, and she reached out in the darkness to set the switch on her alarm clock. It would never do for her to oversleep tomorrow morning.

Sandra groaned and turned over in her sleep. It couldn't be morning yet, but somebody was up—making noise. *Thump!* She sat up in bed, wide awake now. There were more noises. It sounded as though someone was walking around in the living room, bumping into things, opening and closing doors. Then all at once there was silence.

"Katherine?" Sandra called out.

No answer. Sandra waited a minute and then grudgingly got out of bed. The streetlights shone in through the living room windows so that even without turning on the lights she could see it was empty. But there was a crack of light coming from under the bathroom door. Sandra went to it and knocked. "Katherine?" she said softly. When there was no response she opened the door.

Katherine was there, standing over the sink, gazing spellbound at her reflection in the mirror. In her right hand was the bottle of sleeping pills and in her other hand was an empty glass.

"What are you doing?" Sandra asked sharply.

Katherine did not betray the slightest reaction to her question.

"Answer me," Sandra insisted.

This time Katherine quickly turned and walked out of the bathroom, pushing past Sandra as if she weren't even there. Sandra followed her and watched her sit down on the couch in the dark living room.

She turned on the light and stood in front of her. "Katherine, will you please tell me what you're doing?" she begged.

Katherine set down the empty glass on the table in front of her, but she held on to the bottle of pills. She was not looking at Sandra but at some point on the wall behind her.

Was she sleepwalking? It was possible. Sandra had heard that people sometimes did it with their eyes open.

Then Katherine drew her knee up to her chin and said abruptly, "Did you know that I almost got married once?"

Startled, Sandra did not know whether or not to answer her. But Katherine seemed to be waiting for a reply, so Sandra said, "No, you never told me that."

"Well, it's true," Katherine said, still staring at the wall. "To a boy from Iowa. It's funny, sometimes I can hear the same inflections in your voice. Iowa, Minnesota—they're not that far apart."

"No. No, they're not," Sandra said. She pulled up a chair and sat down. She was struck by the disparity between the dazed expression on Katherine's face and the coherence in her words.

"Would you like to know how I met him?" Katherine asked.

"Sure. Anything you want to tell me."

"It was a long time ago—ten years, to be exact. Sometimes I forget how long ago it really was, because I can remember it so much better than things that happened just a year or two ago."

"That's the way it is when things make a strong impression on you," Sandra agreed.

Katherine did not seem to have heard her. "It was the happiest time of my life," she said sadly. "I was twenty, and I had just graduated from Smith. I'd done really well there, and I was all set up to go to Columbia in the fall. I wanted to become a lady journalist and I was dying to work on a newspaper that summer. So my parents sent me out to work on one of my mother's brother's newspapers in Iowa—Ames. I knew I'd get more experience there than if I worked on a paper in the city. So I let my parents do that for me—because that was what I wanted to do.

"And it was wonderful. I got to do everything: police reporting, social news, farm stories, features—just anything that came along. So, on one assignment I had to go over to the university—"

"Iowa State," Sandra interjected.

"I forgot you'd know that," Katherine said. Then she went on with her story: "I don't even particularly remember what the assignment was about, but I had to interview someone in the engineering department, and I remember wondering to myself, *What kind of people study engineering?* Anyway, I found the office where I had to go, and when I walked in there was this boy sitting there. He smiled at me, and it was the nicest smile I'd ever seen. He turned out to be a graduate student, and he answered all my questions—very seriously. He didn't even laugh when I asked him some dumb ones." A smile flickered across her face, then quickly disappeared. "We started dating, a couple of nights a week at first, but pretty soon it became an every night thing."

"What did your aunt and uncle think of that?" Sandra asked.

"My—oh, they don't live there. He owns a lot of newspapers," Katherine explained. "This was just one of them. So I was by myself—more or less. I suppose everybody at the paper was watching over me. I stayed in a rooming house, so Jim— that was his name—had no idea about my family. That was very important to me."

"But didn't you tell him?"

"Of course, I told him—later. When I was sure that it was me he was interested in—not my family's money. When he—" Katherine's voice cracked, "when he asked me to marry him, that was when I told him."

"Did you tell him you'd marry him?"

"Of course. I was crazy about him. I'd never met anyone like him before. He was so *untainted,* so different from the boys I'd known all my life— they were all jaded by the time they were thirteen. Maybe compared to them he was a little naïve, but he was just as bright as they were. He was idealistic and passionate, curious about everything, and *happy.*" She paused, then said wistfully, "And sex. Up until then sex had been something that I tried to avoid whenever I could, but with him I couldn't get enough of it."

Her tone changed, became almost bitter. "I met his mother. She was a widow and he was an only child. He wanted to meet my family, so I brought him home with me at the end of the summer. My parents never gave him a chance. He wasn't 'our kind'; he was Catholic; and his future was limited.

"After Jim left, my parents and I quarreled over him. No, not my parents—my *father*. My mother never said a word. But my father was absolutely livid over the idea of my marrying Jim. We fought constantly about it, right up to the minute I went off to Columbia. After that, things calmed down for a while, simply because my father and I didn't see each other. Then, I was supposed to visit Jim at Christmas, but my father forbade it, and they dragged me off to go skiing in Switzerland. It was a horrible holiday. My father and I barely spoke to each other, and I would have gone out of my mind if it hadn't been for the skiing. But by the end of the trip I thought my father had begun to soften about Jim. I was wrong.

"Three weeks later he called me down to his office and showed me this folder. It was all about Jim—he had had him *investigated*. When he started reading me some of the stuff—like how Jim's father had been an alcoholic and drank himself to death—I got so disgusted I ran out of his office.

"Then I didn't hear from him for a while, until several weeks later he summoned me down to his office again. This time he asked me if I was still determined to marry Jim. When I said yes, he took out a whole pile of legal forms and shoved them under my nose. He told me that those papers gave him absolute power over me until I was twenty-one—which I would turn in a few months —and after that if I still refused to obey him, he would cut off all my money and I wouldn't be able to touch my trust funds until I was twenty-five. I just laughed at him, and that was a big mistake. He got red in the face, and I thought he was going to hit me—again. But then he said—so quietly that it really scared me—that if I married Jim, he would see to it that Jim never got a decent job in any company in this country. And I knew he could do it. One word from him and Jim's career would be ruined—no executive would dare hire Jim against the great Philip Fielding's wishes. That shook me—more than his threats against me.

"After that I agonized for weeks about what to do, until I finally realized that I had to break up with Jim. I kept telling myself that maybe in time my father would mellow, but that now I couldn't risk it—for Jim's sake. So I called Jim and told him that it was all over, I had changed my mind. I couldn't bring myself to tell him the real reason. I felt like such a coward—backing down to my father like that, but I didn't know what else to do.

"Jim seemed to take it well—at first. I suppose he was expecting it. But then he started writing to me and calling me all the time, begging to come out and see me so we could talk things over. I knew I couldn't bear to see him again, so the more he pushed, the more I resisted. Finally, I guess I said some pretty harsh things to him because I didn't hear from him for a while. In the meantime, I'd gotten my first job on a magazine and my own apartment and I was feeling kind of cocky, glad to be independent of my parents for the first time in my life. I didn't like what I'd done to Jim, but I didn't see any other way of handling it. So I was surprised when I got another letter from him—I hadn't heard from him in several weeks—and the letter seemed so sad, so unlike Jim. He told me that several times he had gotten in his car, thinking he would just drive to New York to see me, no matter what I said. But after he'd gone fifty or sixty miles he realized how foolish he was being and how hopeless it was, so he had turned his car around and gone back home. That letter disturbed me a lot and I almost called him, but in the end I decided not to. Then about ten days later I got another letter. Only it wasn't from Jim—it was from his mother." Katherine's voice faltered. "She—she said Jim was dead. He'd smashed up his car on a highway in Illinois."

"Oh, no!" Sandra burst out.

Katherine nodded gravely. "She said nobody could figure out what he was doing on the highway—or even how the accident happened—he'd gone straight into a tree at seventy miles an hour."

Sandra shuddered. "My God!"

Katherine ignored her. "But she said *she* knew what he was doing there—and why it happened. And then she told me that she hoped I rotted in hell for what I had done to him." Her voice began rising in pitch. "And that as far as she was concerned, Jim hadn't killed himself, *I* had. I was his murderer!"

Katherine's hands were shaking so violently

that Sandra could hear the capsules in the pill bottle rattling against each other. But her face still showed no emotion.

"That must have upset you a great deal," Sandra said gently.

Katherine blinked. "That's putting it mildly. I was hysterical. Having Jim dead was awful enough—but then to have his mother accuse me of—" The words died in her throat. "I was beside myself. So I called a friend of mine from graduate school and she came over and brought some tranquilizers with her. She stayed with me until I was finally calm enough to go to sleep and then she went home. That night—for the first time in years—I had the nightmare again. Only it was much, much worse this time—because instead of my father, the man in it was Jim!" She covered her eyes with her hand. "It woke me up, of course, and I was in an even worse state than I was before. So I decided to take some more tranquilizers, only there was just one left in the bottle. But that gave me an idea, and first thing in the morning I took the empty bottle to the pharmacy on the label and had it refilled. Then I went home and took the whole bottle."

Sandra held her breath. She suddenly understood the point of the story.

Katherine sighed and took her hand away from her eyes. "But I didn't die, of course. My friend was worried about me, and she called my office. When they told her I wasn't in and they hadn't heard from me, she called me at home but I'd taken the phone off the hook. So she came over and got the super to let her in. I guess they found me just in time. I had my stomach pumped, and they called my parents from the hospital. When I came to, they were both there, and my mother was hovering over me—in her sable coat—and my father was ordering people around in his usual, arrogant way. I could barely look at him.

"That was the last time I ever saw him. From that moment on I decided that whatever I did I would have nothing to do with him—or his money. That's why I've never touched my trust funds. I pretend they're not there. I don't even know how much is in them anymore. I guess they just sit there, making money." Katherine shrugged. "I don't care. The only money that matters to me is the money I make myself." Her tone was defiant.

"Anyway, I survived the overdose of tranquilizers, but my friend insisted that I go into therapy —that was when I started seeing a shrink."

Suddenly Sandra remembered the pained reference Philip Fielding had made to an earlier breakdown. So this is what he was talking about, Sandra realized, Katherine's nearly successful suicide attempt. And now she was thinking of trying it again.

"Katherine," she said cautiously, "what were you doing with those pills when I found you?"

Katherine looked at the pills as if she had never seen them before. "These? I don't know. Maybe nothing." Then she added darkly, "Maybe not."

Sandra held out her hand. "Give them to me."

"No." Katherine clutched the bottle to her chest. "They're mine. I need them."

"I'll give them to you when you have to take

them," Sandra said very deliberately. "But I want the bottle."

"I won't take them all, I promise." Katherine's voice was high, whiny—like a child's.

"I believe you," Sandra said. "Just give me the bottle." Her hand was still extended, unwavering.

Katherine's eyes flashed a challenge and then she hurled the bottle at Sandra.

Bending over to retrieve it, Sandra said, "Thank you."

"You're welcome!" Katherine shouted, jumping up from the couch.

Sandra's head jerked up. "Where are you going?"

"Back to bed! I know I can't sleep, but I'm not going to sit here and look at your smug face any longer!" With that, Katherine was gone, slamming her bedroom door behind her.

Sandra winced at the sound. Then it was quiet again. She continued to sit there, turning the bottle of sleeping pills over and over in her hand. Finally, she switched off the lights and went back to her own room. It was many hours later when she managed to fall asleep.

When her alarm jarred her awake, Sandra opened her eyes groggily. She couldn't remember what day it was. Did she have to get up? Oh, yes, this was Tuesday—maybe she'd call in sick. Then she remembered Stan, and she sat up. She *had* to go to work—it would look suspicious otherwise. If neither of them came in, people might assume they were together. Well, Stan wouldn't be coming in

—that was for sure. She just hoped he hadn't told anyone about their date. Somehow she doubted that he had. He had meant for them to have a long-term thing and it would have spoiled it if somebody else knew about them.

She got out of bed and went into the bathroom, relieved to see that Katherine wasn't up yet. That meant she could have the extra time in the bathroom that she needed. She had to make a special effort today with both her hair and her makeup— so that nobody could tell how tired and worried she was. After showering, she dried her hair and put on her makeup, carefully covering the dark circles under her eyes.

When she left the bathroom to go into her own room to finish dressing, she knocked on Katherine's door. Hearing a muffled response from inside, she opened it. Katherine was lying in bed, looking much as she had last night when they arrived home. Her eyes were wide-open, but blank, staring up at the ceiling.

"Why aren't you up?" Sandra asked.

Katherine shut her eyes and then slowly opened them. "Because I'm not going to work."

Sandra hesitated. "Do you want me to tell them you're sick?"

"I don't care. Tell them anything. It doesn't matter anymore."

"Katherine," Sandra said sympathetically, "I know how you feel."

"No, you don't. You don't have the vaguest idea of how I feel. No one does." Katherine turned over with her back to Sandra.

"All right," Sandra sighed. "I'll call you later."

She didn't even bother to buy the papers, she was so sure that Stan had not been found. On the bus she considered every detail the police would find when Stan's body was discovered: a naked, middle-aged man lying face down in the bedroom, with several stab wounds in his back and his own belt nearby. They would find no fingerprints on the dresser or the doorknobs of the bathroom and bedroom, and all the surfaces in the bathroom would be wiped clean. Actually, this one had been much easier to clean up than Ted Hanley's murder: there had been so much more blood then. But except for a slight stain on Katherine's sweater and a few spots on her own dress, there had been little blood.

When she got into the office she called Vivian and told her to report Katherine sick for the day, that she had the flu. Five minutes after she hung up the phone, Vivian came into the library and shut the door behind her.

"Okay, Sandra," she said, folding her arms in a determined way across her chest, "level with me. Don't give me any of this bullshit about the flu. I want you to tell me what's really wrong with Katie."

"I don't know what you're talking about," Sandra said, icily. She didn't like the tone of Vivian's voice.

Vivian leaned over Sandra's desk. "Don't play dumb with *me*," she said. "You and I both know what's been going on, only I think you know a lot more than I do."

Sandra felt fear grip her heart. This was something she had dreaded; Vivian was too close to the truth. "Don't you think you might be jumping to conclusions?" she asked, trying to keep her voice calm.

"No, I don't," Vivian said harshly. "I've seen the way Katie's been acting lately—something's wrong. She doesn't confide in me anymore, but I know she'd tell *you* what's bothering her."

Relief flooded over Sandra. Vivian didn't know anything, she was just guessing. And she was jealous, envious that Sandra had replaced her as Katherine's closest friend. "Oh, well, you're right," Sandra said vaguely. "She *does* have something on her mind. But I don't know what it is, she won't tell me. That's why I think she caught the flu though—because she's been so run down."

Vivian cocked an eyebrow. "I don't believe you. But if that's the way you want it," she said, "I'll just have to call Katie myself." She jerked the door open and stormed out of the library.

Sandra immediately picked up the phone and dialed her own number.

The phone rang and rang, and with each ring Sandra could feel her throat tightening. There was a phone right by Katherine's bed, why didn't she answer? Then someone picked up and a faint voice said, "Hello?"

"Where were you?" Sandra rasped.

"Right here."

"Why did it take you so long to answer the phone?"

"I didn't hear it."

Sandra let that pass. "Listen," she said, "I told Vivian that you have the flu. So if she calls, that's what you tell her."

There was no sound from the other end.

"Did you hear me?" Sandra asked.

"Uh-huh," came the lethargic reply. "If anybody calls, I've got the flu."

"Right. Don't tell her anything else—no matter what she says. Do you understand? I'll call you later to see how you are."

"Okay."

Sandra hung up. She would give Katherine another hour or two and then call back. Trying to keep her mind occupied, she let herself get caught up in the routine of the library until midmorning. She was about to reach for the phone to call Katherine again, when it rang.

"Library," she answered in a perfunctory voice.

"Miss Jurgenson, this is Philip Fielding."

*Oh, no, not now,* Sandra thought. "Hello. How are you?" she asked.

"Well, I've been worried." There was real urgency in his voice. "Why haven't I heard from you?"

"I'm sorry," she said. "Actually, I was going to call you today—but I guess I dreaded doing it."

"Why? What's happened?" he asked desperately.

"Things are much worse than I thought."

"Oh, my God. How bad is it?"

"Bad enough for her to stay home today." Sandra lowered her voice. "I've told everyone she has the flu—but that's not the case."

"I've got to see her! I'm going over there—"

"No!" Sandra cut in. "That's the worst thing you could do."

"But I can't just sit by while she—" His voice

broke off, and Sandra thought she heard a muffled sob on the other end of the phone.

"You've got to leave this up to me," Sandra said soothingly. "You can't—well, I think you know how she feels about you. Anything you did would only make it worse—for both of you."

"But what are *you* going to do?"

"That I don't know—just yet. But she trusts me, and I think she'll listen to me. Maybe not right now, but eventually."

"Oh, God, I hope so."

"Mr. Fielding, don't worry. You can trust me, too. I know what I'm doing."

"All right," he said reluctantly. "I guess I'm forced to rely on your judgment. But, *please*, keep me informed."

"I promise. If anything happens, I'll call you right away."

Sandra hung up the phone, feeling almost smug about the way she had handled him. Poor man. His precious daughter is practically a basket case. But she would be there to help him forget Katherine.

She looked down at her hands. They were covered with black ink, smudges from the newsprint she had been handling all morning. Locking the library, she went into the ladies' room to wash her hands.

The receptionist, the one who had teased her about the flowers, was there, patching up her makeup. Sandra glanced at her and gave her the barest smile.

The girl nodded and went back to dabbing at her eye shadow, but spoke to Sandra's image in the mirror. "Have you heard about Mr. Herzberg?" she asked.

Sandra dropped her eyes and pretended to be absorbed in scrubbing her hands. "No. What?" she said casually.

"He's missing," the girl said, smiling wickedly.

Sandra looked at her in the mirror. "Missing?"

"Well, his wife doesn't know where he is, that's for sure," the girl laughed. "She's been calling here all morning, and when he didn't show up for work she started calling Mr. Roth. She told him she hasn't heard from him since yesterday and he never came home last night."

"Where'd you hear all this?" Sandra asked coolly.

"From Ellie. Who else?"

"Well, what does Charles—Mr. Roth—think about this?"

The girl shrugged. "Nothing. He told Ellie Mr. Herzberg probably spent the night with some woman and that he'll most likely show up later in the day."

"I wonder what he told Mrs. Herzberg," Sandra mused.

"Oh, he covered up for him. He told her that her husband was working on a special project and that he probably stayed late at the office and then just went to a hotel and overslept this morning."

"Men!" Sandra sneered, turning off the water and drying her hands. "They sure do stick together, don't they?"

"Guess so," the girl responded, more interested now in applying her mascara than gossiping.

Sandra left the ladies' room feeling strangely

excited. How long would it be before anybody realized that Stan was never going to show up? And even when they did, what would they do about it?

Yes, it was very exciting being right on the scene like this—but it was also dangerous.

Philip Fielding paced back and forth in front of his windows, not seeing the magnificent view spread out below him. All he could see was Katherine, the one thing he truly loved in this world. Ever since she had been born, he had lived only for her. His wife, his son—yes, he loved them, too. But not like Katherine.

She had been a perfect baby and then the most beautiful little girl, and everything had been so wonderful between them for all those early years. She adored him and had been so proud of the fact that she looked just like him. But suddenly things changed. She started becoming a woman, and every time he looked at her he would feel terrible, unnatural desires. Something would break inside him then, and he would have to punish her for what she aroused in him. That was when he had begun losing her.

But the worst thing had been over that worthless boy. The nerve of him, wanting to marry Katherine. It had made his flesh crawl, just thinking of that boy running his hands over Katherine's body, making love to her. No, he could never allow that. Katherine would marry someday, but not to some puny guttersnipe. He could never let her waste herself on someone like that. So he had prevented the marriage. But the boy—that stupid, weak-willed boy—he went and killed himself. And then—oh, God, it still hurt him to think of it—Katherine had tried to kill herself, too.

That was when he really lost her. He was sure that Katherine blamed *him* for the boy's death. Her eyes had told him that as she lay on her hospital bed, staring hatefully up at him. But she had never told him so. Because she had not spoken to him since. No matter how he tried, she would not see him.

Ten years—it had been ten years since he had seen his daughter's face. Or even heard her voice.

No more, no more. He couldn't stand it any longer. He *must* talk to her. He walked over to his desk and extended his hand toward the telephone. He didn't care what her roommate said, he was going to call his daughter. She needed him—and he needed her.

He had almost finished dialing the number when he realized he didn't know what to say to Katherine. What do you say after ten years? And what if she hung up on him? Or what if he upset her so much that she did something irrational?

Trembling, he put down the phone. He didn't dare risk it. He'd have to leave Katherine in Sandra Jurgenson's hands.

## CHAPTER TWELVE

Wednesday mornings were usually the best part of the week for Lucia Osorio. The apartment she had to clean then was the easiest one on her list. There was never anybody there, and sometimes it looked like no one had been there since the Wednesday before, and that made her job very simple.

She unlocked the door and stepped inside. *¡Que estraño!* The lights were on. "Hallo?" she cried out. "Is Mrs. Osorio." No answer. She shrugged, took off her coat and hung it up in the closet. Then she spied the broken glass on the floor. *¡Ay! Que sucio son.* And, of course, whoever had broken it hadn't bothered to clean it up. They had left that for her to do. They'd probably tracked glass into the rug, too. She went into the kitchen, got out the broom and dustpan and carefully swept up all the fragments. After she'd deposited them in the garbage pail, she glanced around the kitchen. She was positive that it hadn't been used since she last cleaned it. So all she'd have to do was vacuum the floor, then do the living room, and after that go on to the bathroom and bedroom.

Mrs. Osorio spent the next twenty minutes busily running the vacuum cleaner through the kitch-

en and living room. When she was finished, she
shut the machine off, wiped her face, and then
walked straight down the hall to the bathroom.

The lights were on here, too. The room was spot-
less, but someone had used all the towels. They
were hanging rumpled and askew on the towel
racks. Mrs. Osorio pulled them down and threw
them over her arm. Then she stepped across the
hall to the bedroom. The door was shut, and she
pushed it open.

The putrid smell reached her nostrils before
she saw the horror on the floor. When her eyes
registered what it was, she backed out of the room,
screaming, the towels flying from her arms as she
ran along the hall, across the living room, out
through the door, and into the lobby, still screaming. She could hear footsteps rushing down the
stairs, so she ran toward them. Halfway up the
stairs she met a man she recognized as another
tenant. "What is it?" he shouted, catching her by
the shoulders.

"¡Un muerto!" Mrs. Osorio screamed.

"What? What?" the man said, shaking her
gently. "Speak English, I can't understand you!"

"A man—dead!" Mrs. Osorio moaned and closed
her eyes.

The man looked at her sharply. "Where?"

She pointed down the stairs.

"Stay here. I'll go see."

Mrs. Osorio sank down on the stairs while the
man pushed past her. He went across the lobby
and into the apartment.

In a minute he came out, his face ashen, and

took Mrs. Osorio by the arm. "Come up to my apartment," he said. "We have to call the police."

Frank MacLaughlin dropped to one knee beside the body, his eyes taking in everything: the wounds in the back, all seven of them; the head twisted to the right as if the man had been trying to look over his shoulder; the man's belt lying on the floor, partially under the body.

"See what I mean, Frank?" a detective said behind him. "Same damn thing."

"Yeah," MacLaughlin said, rising to his feet. "Who is this guy?"

"Nobody in the building has ever seen him before," the detective answered. "We got a wallet out of the clothes over there." He indicated the pile on the floor. "Driver's license says Stanley D. Herzberg, age forty-two. The description fits him. It's a Mamaroneck address."

"Who found him?"

"Cleaning woman. The upstairs neighbor heard her screaming and came down to check it out. He's the one who phoned us. They're upstairs now."

"Okay, I'll go see them." MacLaughlin turned to go, then stopped. "Has anybody notified Mamaroneck? We need a positive I.D. on this guy."

"It's already been taken care of," the detective assured him.

The cleaning woman and the neighbor were cooperative, but they couldn't add much to what the police already knew. The cleaning woman swore that she had never seen the man before. He could be her employer, but she wasn't sure because she had never seen him either. She had been hired by a secretary and received her monthly checks through the mail. When MacLaughlin asked her who signed the checks, she got flustered and said she couldn't remember. MacLaughlin let it go. That could be checked later.

The neighbor, too, denied knowing the victim. As far as he knew, no one lived in that apartment. But he did recall that on several occasions he had seen a man—not this man—leaving or entering the apartment, and he had been accompanied by a different young woman each time.

MacLaughlin left them and went back downstairs to the murder scene. The lab men were busy checking for fingerprints, but he doubted that they would find any. This killer was too smart for that. But somewhere along the line she would have to slip up, and MacLaughlin planned to be there when she did. So far, he had not been able to find the connection between the killer and Ted Hanley. Now he had another victim, more leads to follow. Maybe somewhere they intersected, and at the crossroads he would find her.

Louise Herzberg puffed so hard on the cigarette that the cords in her neck stood out in sharp definition. MacLaughlin watched her, hoping she hadn't been so shaken by the ordeal of identifying her husband's body that she couldn't answer his questions.

She exhaled with a force that shot the smoke

out like a missile. "What happened to him?" she asked brusquely.

"He was stabbed, Mrs. Herzberg," MacLaughlin said as tactfully as he could.

She blinked. "Who did it?"

"We don't know that yet," MacLaughlin said. "But we're working on it."

"Was he mugged?"

"No, nothing was taken that we could see—although we'll want you to go through the effects."

She nodded sadly and averted her eyes. She had seemed haggard when he first saw her, but now she appeared to be completely drained, and looked much older than her thirty-eight or thirty-nine years. She was expensively dressed and her brown hair was freshly coiffed, and MacLaughlin guessed that she was probably pretty. But it was impossible to see that now, her face was so ravaged by pain.

"I have to ask you a few questions," he said gently.

She looked up. "Wait—I have to know. Where did it happen?"

MacLaughlin described the details of the murder scene to her, softening his words. But he could see by her face that the fact that her husband must have been involved in a sexual encounter when he met his death had not escaped her.

"Mrs. Herzberg," he said, "the belt is significant."

"How?"

"Because we think it may have been part of a sadomasochistic sexual practice—"

"Not Stan," she burst out. "He wouldn't—he *couldn't*—do anything like that!"

"We're not saying that he did, Mrs. Herzberg. It may have been done to him—or he may have been forced to go along."

"Dear God!" she said in a choked voice. Nervous fingers flew to her hair, leaving it wild and disheveled.

"Do you know who lives in that apartment?" MacLaughlin asked.

"No, I haven't the vaguest idea. Don't you know?"

"We're running that down now."

She ground out her cigarette in an ashtray. "I just don't know," she murmured. "Who could have done this—and *why*?" Her dark eyes fixed on his, pressing for the answer to her question.

He tried to meet her gaze, but his own eyes wavered. He had seen that look so many times, and it always unnerved him. He cleared his throat. "We don't know that for sure," he said, hating the inadequacy of his words, "but we do have a lead."

"A lead?" she echoed.

"Yes. It's a case I've been working on—the details are very similar."

Her eyes narrowed. "You mean whoever did this to my husband has done it before?"

"We think so."

"But why haven't you found him? Why didn't you catch him before he—" Her voice broke.

"Actually, Mrs. Herzberg, we think it's a woman."

"A woman?" she gasped. "A woman did this to Stan?"

MacLaughlin nodded.

She stared at him, shaking her head in disbelief.

He leaned forward. His ruse had failed. She obviously didn't know about any other woman in her husband's life. If she had, she would have denounced her on the spot. "I don't mean to push you, Mrs. Herzberg, but I do need to ask you some questions about your husband."

"He's dead," she said listlessly. "Isn't that all you need to know?"

MacLaughlin sighed. "We want to find his killer. By checking into your husband's background we may come across a connection—something that will lead us to the killer."

"What kind of things do you want to know?"

"His friends, acquaintances, business dealings, habits, things like that."

"Well, I guess I can help you with some of that," she said reluctantly. "But you'd better talk to Charles about the business stuff."

"Charles?"

"Charles Roth. He's head of Roth Publishing. My husband worked there—he was vice-president in charge of circulation. He's been there a long time, and he and Charles were good friends."

"Fine," MacLaughlin said, noting it down. He looked at his watch. Nearly four o'clock—he'd never make it there today. He'd have to save Roth Publishing for tomorrow.

"I'm sick about this—just sick," Charles Roth said, rubbing his eyes. "I didn't get any sleep last night after I heard what happened to poor Stan. I still can't believe it." He looked across his desk at MacLaughlin, and slowly shook his head.

MacLaughlin tapped his pencil against his notebook. "Mr. Roth," he said, "when did you last see Mr. Herzberg?"

"Monday—in the afternoon. I just saw him for a few minutes."

"How did he seem?"

"Fine."

"Did he say where he was going after work?"

"No. I assumed he was going home."

"Did you notice anything ususual in his behavior?"

Charles hesitated. "He did seem kind of nervous."

"In what way?"

"Well, it was like he wasn't quite there. When I was talking to him I got the feeling he wasn't paying attention—he was thinking about something else."

"Do you have any idea what that might have been?"

"I couldn't say for certain—but I think it might have been a woman."

"Why is that?"

"Because I've known—I knew—Stan for a long time. He was very cool about anything to do with business, nothing rattled him. But women were something else."

"Can you be more specific?"

Charles leaned back in his chair and swiveled it to the side so that he wasn't facing the detective directly. "Don't get me wrong," he said. "Stan was happily married. But I don't think he was completely faithful to Louise—he did his share of playing around."

"Did he tell you this?"

"No, not in so many words. It's just a feeling I have." Charles turned his chair slightly and looked at the detective. "Stan wasn't one to brag about things like that. But I'm pretty sure he had an affair with one of the secretaries here."

"Who is that?"

"She's not here anymore," Charles said with a wave of his hand. "I don't even remember her name, but you could look it up in Personnel. That was a couple of years ago, anyway."

"Have there been any others that you know of?"

"No," Charles said pensively. Then a light dawned in his eyes. "Maybe I shouldn't say this— it's just a hunch."

"What is it?"

"Well," Charles said, "it just seemed funny to me. There's this girl here—she's really beautiful in a cold sort of way—but one time Stan complained to me about what a bitch she was. And then a few days later he made a point of telling me he'd changed his mind about her, he decided she was really nice after all. I thought to myself then that he was on the make for her."

"What's her name?"

"Katherine Fielding," Charles said cautiously. "Are you going to question her?"

"Of course. We have to question everyone."

"Then you'd better go easy on her. Her father's got a lot of clout with City Hall. I don't think he'd like it if his daughter were harassed by the police."

"I'm not going to harass her," MacLaughlin said dryly. "I just want to ask her a few questions."

Vivian looked up as the strange man appeared in the doorway. He was in his thirties, but still boyish-looking, with sandy brown hair and a handsome Irish face. She knew right away he was a detective.

"Yes?" she said. "Can I help you?"

"I'm Detective MacLaughlin," he said, reaching into his pocket for his badge.

"You don't have to show me that," she said quickly. "I already heard that there were two detectives here asking everyone questions about Stan."

"Good, that eliminates the preliminaries," he said, taking out a notebook and pencil. "Could I have your name, please?"

"Browne—with an 'e.' Vivian Browne."

"Is that Miss or Mrs.?"

"Neither," she said matter-of-factly.

"Date of birth?"

"August 10, 1943."

"How long have you worked here, Ms. Browne?"

"A little over two years."

"Did you know Mr. Herzberg well?"

"No—not very."

She had been straightforward enough, but MacLaughlin had caught a flicker of something—Fear? Caution?—in her eyes. He pointed casually in the direction of the empty desk across the room. "Does anyone sit there?" he asked.

"Yes, but she's out sick."

"What's her name?"

"Katherine Fielding."

"How long has she been out?"

"Uh, since Tuesday. She's got the flu."

"Was she friendly with Mr. Herzberg?"

Vivian moistened her lips and regarded him steadily. "Well, yes, sort of. He came to see her a lot. You know, he'd just hang around and talk to her."

MacLaughlin lowered his voice. "This is an awkward question, but I have to ask it. Were they having an affair?"

Vivian's head jerked up proudly. "Of course not! There was nothing between them. Katherine was just pleasant to him. I think she felt sorry for him."

"Why was that?"

"How should I know?"

"Okay. Now how do I get in touch with her?"

"I—why don't you ask her roommate? She works here, too."

"What's her name?"

"Sandra Jurgenson. She works in the library."

"All right, I'll do that. Thank you for your help, Ms. Browne." She looked for a moment as if she were about to say something, then thought the better of it. MacLaughlin turned to go, but as he went through the door he glanced back over his shoulder. She was reaching for the phone.

Sandra jumped when the phone rang. "Library."

"Sandra, it's Vivian." Her voice sounded anxious. "Listen, one of those detectives was just here to see me. He was asking a lot of questions about Katherine and Stan, and he wanted to know how to get in touch with her. So I told him to ask you. I figured you'd know how to handle him better than I." The last few words were said sarcastically.

"Yeah, sure," Sandra said. "Thanks a lot. She's not in any condition to see the police. I'll have to put him off."

Vivian hesitated. "Sandra?"

"Yes?"

"*Was* there anything between them?"

"Not that I know of."

"I've been so worried about her—ever since last night when I heard about Stan. I just kept thinking about how strange she's been lately and that she hasn't been to work since Tuesday and Stan has been missing since then."

"What are you trying to say, Vivian?"

"I don't know. I guess maybe I'm just scared for her—that maybe she was with him or she knows something about what happened to him."

"Vivian, she's got the *flu*, she's sick as a dog. She didn't know about Stan until I saw it on the news last night and told her. She was just as shocked as I was."

"All right. Don't mind me. It's that damn detective. He gave me the jitters."

Sandra only dimly heard Vivian's words. Her eyes had fastened on the library door, watching, waiting. "Listen, I better go," she blurted out. "I'll talk to you later."

She put down the phone, feeling sick in the pit of her stomach. She didn't want to see any detective, or answer his questions. She wanted to run out of the library, go someplace safe. Only there was no place like that—not anymore.

She had known this was going to happen today and she had wanted to stay home, be catatonic like Katherine. But she knew they would find her there. So she had come to work, trying to give the appearance of normality.

Not that it mattered. The whole company was stunned and talking of nothing but Stan's murder. And then the word had gone around that two detectives were asking questions. Charles wanted everyone to cooperate with them, tell them anything that might help find Stan's killer.

Sandra shivered. Stan's killer. *Stan's killer*. The words echoed in her mind, but they had no meaning. Surely they did not apply to her. She had never killed anyone, never meant to, anyway. Somehow it had just happened. No, it was Katherine who had killed him—she had just finished off what Katherine started. She had done what Katherine wanted her to do. She had done what needed to be done—for Katherine!

"Are you Sandra Jurgenson?" a masculine voice asked.

Sandra looked up. The man's face seemed vaguely familiar—she was sure she had seen it somewhere before. "Yes," she answered.

"I'm Detective MacLaughlin." He flashed a badge at her. "I'd like to ask you a few questions."

"Sit down." She pointed to a chair.

He drew the chair up to her desk and sat down. She thought he was attractive. Certainly more attractive than the cop she had made a conquest of. My God! What if it had been the same one? A

shiver coursed through her. She glanced up quickly to see if he had noticed, but he was preoccupied
with his notebook.

"How do you spell your name?" he asked, his
pencil poised.

"J-u-r-g-e-n-s-o-n. Sandra."

"Miss or Mrs?"

"Mrs. I'm divorced."

"Date of birth?"

"May 27, 1949."

"How long have you worked here?"

"Close to a year. Ten months, I think."

"Did you know Mr. Herzberg?"

Sandra felt herself go cold. "Yes," she managed
to say in an even voice. "We were fairly friendly."

"When did you last see him?"

"Monday—like everyone else."

"I understand you have a roommate, a Katherine Fielding?"

"Yes, she works here, too. But she's out sick."

"I'd like to ask her some questions, just routine,
you understand. Where can I reach her?"

Sandra's heart skipped a beat, but she hoped
her face showed nothing. "I don't think you can
right now. She's really too sick to talk to you."

"What's wrong with her?"

"The flu. She's had it for several days now, and
she's very weak."

"It would only take a minute," he persisted.
"I'll just call her. What's the number?"

Sandra panicked. "No, really you shouldn't,"
she said, too quickly. "I'll tell you what, though.
When I see her tonight, I'll tell her that you want

to talk to her. Then when she's up to it, she can call you herself."

MacLaughlin didn't bat an eyelash. "All right," he said, and handed her a scrap of paper. "Here's the number." He stood up. "Tell her to do it soon." And he walked out.

He didn't believe me, Sandra thought. He suspects something and he can go straight to Personnel and get our phone number and address. *I've got to get out of here right away!*

She grabbed her coat and threw it over her shoulders, her mind racing wildly. What if the detective got to Katherine before she did? All he had to do was push her a little and Katherine would fall apart, confess everything.

Should she call Philip Fielding and tell him to use his influence to keep the police away from Katherine? No, she would have to explain too much, and even he could not keep the police at bay forever. No, she would have to take care of this alone. Somehow she must do something to convince the police that Katherine was so crazy she could not be believed.

She hurried downstairs and hailed a taxi. They took off up Madison, but the driver could not go fast enough for her. "Get going," she urged him when they appeared to be dawdling in traffic. "It's an emergency!"

When they pulled up in front of her building, she thrust a five-dollar bill into the driver's hand and jumped out, not bothering with the change. She wanted to break into a run, but forced herself into a rapid stride, nodded to the doorman as he opened the door, and continued across the lobby to the elevators.

She had to wait briefly, and as she cursed the delay, another woman walked up, pulling a heavily loaded shopping cart. When the elevator came, Sandra stepped in and pushed the button for the fourteenth floor, willing the elevator door to close before the other woman could get in. But she pulled her cart in and pressed the button for eight. Sandra counted the floors as they ascended. It seemed to be taking forever. They stopped at eight, and Sandra could have strangled the woman as she struggled clumsily with her cart, catching it on the door, and then finally pushing it free. At last the door closed and the elevator crawled up the remaining flights. When she reached fourteen, Sandra could contain herself no longer. She sprinted down the hallway, quickly unlocked their door and stepped inside, panting.

Their apartment was absolutely still. Sandra tiptoed across the living room to Katherine's door. It was standing ajar and she cautiously peeked around it. Katherine appeared to be asleep. Sandra had left two pills for her in the morning. They were no longer on the night table. She breathed a sigh of relief. She was safe—for the moment—but time was running out. She had to do something. And fast. Going to her own room, she struggled out of her coat and sat down on the bed. Her mind was a jumble. Then slowly, haltingly, a plan began to shape itself out of the chaos.

"Katherine, wake up!" she barked. She was standing over Katherine's bed, shaking her.

Still asleep, Katherine tried to turn away from the intrusion.

Sandra pinned her down and shook her again, more roughly this time. "Wake up!" she said, her voice louder, more insistent.

Katherine's eyes opened halfway. "Who is it?" she said drowsily.

"It's Sandra."

"Oh." She closed her eyes again.

Sandra grabbed her shoulder, shaking her until her eyes flew open. "Katherine, listen to me," she shouted. "Have there been any phone calls? Any at all?"

"No. Why?" Katherine asked, sitting up.

"Because I have some very bad news for you, Katherine," Sandra said ominously. "I think you're going to get a phone call from the police this afternoon. That's why I came home—to warn you."

All the color drained out of Katherine's face, and the muscles in it went so rigid that her skin appeared to be made of pale, brittle porcelain. Her dazed, frightened eyes were fixed on Sandra's.

Sandra stared back at her, hard, unrelenting. "They know, Katherine," she said. "They know."

"What am I going to do?" The appeal in Katherine's voice was desperate.

"I don't know," Sandra said coldly. "I can't help you anymore." Then she added bitterly, "And I don't want to—not after last night."

Katherine's expression was stricken. "Last night?" she said pathetically. "What happened last night?"

Sandra took a step back as if protecting herself from Katherine. "You mean you don't remember?"

Katherine pressed her hands to her temples. "I —I don't remember anything," she stammered.

"You're lying."

"B—but I'm not. Did I do something?"

"I'll show you what you did," Sandra said, clamping her hand around Katherine's wrist and tugging her out of bed.

"No! No! I don't want to see," Katherine cried. She fell to the floor, clinging to the sheets, her lavender nightgown twisted around her hips.

Sandra gave Katherine's arm a vicious jerk and pulled her, stumbling, to her feet. She was stronger than Katherine and capable of dragging her across the apartment, but it would be easier for her if Katherine walked.

Katherine stumbled again, and this time Sandra did not bother pulling her up but began dragging her across the bedroom floor.

"No! Sandra, don't! Stop!" Katherine begged, grabbing at Sandra's legs, but Sandra kicked her arm away, her furious resolve heightened by Katherine's resistance. She dragged Katherine's thrashing body out of her bedroom, across the width of the living room, and into her own room, where she dropped her arm, leaving her to cry helplessly on the floor.

Breathing heavily, Sandra unbuttoned her blouse and bent over Katherine, gripping her face in her hands. "Look at me," she said hoarsely. "Look at what you tried to do to me!"

Katherine opened her eyes. Slowly they swept down Sandra's face and neck to a bright slash of red on her bared chest. It was an ugly gash that still looked raw. "No!" she screamed and shut her eyes. She clutched frantically at Sandra's arms, trying to wrench them away from her head.

"Oh, no you don't," Sandra cried. "You're going to see the rest of it!" She jerked Katherine's head around so that it was facing her bed. "Open your eyes!" she ordered.

Katherine's eyelids barely separated.

"Look at the bed!" Sandra said, yanking Katherine's head up savagely.

Katherine's eyes bulged as she stared at the bed. The sheets and blanket had been ripped in a long, jagged tear. They were spotted with blood. Just below the pillow, jammed into the mattress, was the bloodstained letter opener. Katherine shrieked and began scratching at Sandra's hands. "Let me go!" she pleaded, digging her nails into Sandra's skin.

Sandra dropped her hands, rubbing the backs of them. "You really love drawing blood, don't you? You murdering bitch!" she spat at Katherine. "But I'm glad they're coming to get you, before you try to kill me again. I'd be dead now, if I hadn't fought you off!"

Katherine covered her ears with her hands. "No! It's not true," she moaned.

"You're insane!" Sandra shouted at her. "Do you hear me? Insane!"

She walked over to the bed and snatched the letter opener out of the mattress. Then she turned on Katherine and brandished it in front of her face. Katherine shrank back, shielding her face with her hands. "Look at this!" Sandra hissed. "You've killed two men with it and then you tried to use it on me. I didn't even know you had it until you attacked me with it. You meant to use it on me all along—that's why you took it away after both murders!"

Katherine's whole body was shivering uncontrollably. "I would never do that to you, Sandra," she said in an anguished voice.

Sandra shook her head violently. "It's no good, Katherine. I can't take it any longer—I'm afraid for my life! It's over and I'm *glad*. Let the police take care of you, I'm through! They'll put you somewhere where you can't hurt anybody anymore!"

Katherine fell back as if Sandra had struck her. "No!" she wailed. "They can't do that!"

"Yes, they can. They will!" Sandra cried. They'll put you away, behind bars because you're hopelessly insane—a homicidal maniac!"

Just then the phone rang, and Sandra pointed in triumph at the extension on her nightstand. "That's the police! And I'm going to tell them to come and get you!"

As Sandra started toward the phone, Katherine sprang at her like an animal and fiercely twisted the letter opener out of her grasp. "Don't touch that phone," she snarled, "or I *will* kill you!" Her eyes were feverish but her hand was steady, the letter opener poised over Sandra's heart.

The phone went on shrilly ringing. Neither woman moved. Their eyes were locked on each other.

It rang for what seemed like an infinity and then, abruptly, it ceased. The only sound in the room was traffic noise filtering up from the street and Katherine's harsh, labored breathing. Slowly, she began backing away from Sandra, holding the letter opener out at arm's length. "Stay away from me," she said in a low, threatening voice. When she reached the door she turned and ran. Sandra could hear her bare feet padding across the living room floor and then the slam of her bedroom door.

Sandra stared after, her mind still seeing the image of Katherine's face, full of unbridled rage, her eyes wild and blazing.

She stood, rooted to the spot, feeling sick fear in the pit of her stomach. It grew, rose up in her throat, and spread over her in cold, numbing waves. Her body sagged and she sank down on her bed, burying her face in her hands. She was physically and emotionally exhausted, too weak even to cry. She had done all she could do—there was nothing left.

## CHAPTER THIRTEEN

She did not know how long she had been sitting there when the phone suddenly started ringing again. She looked up, staring blankly at it as the rings continued, each one more insistent than the last.

Finally it stopped. She sighed and got up wearily. It wasn't over yet, not quite.

She walked unsteadily across the apartment to Katherine's door. Quaking with fear, she turned the doorknob, then took a deep breath and pushed open the door. She couldn't see Katherine at first, so she stepped into the room.

Something was lying near the foot of the bed, but then her vision blurred and she could not make out what it was. She heard a low moan from very far away and somehow knew that the sound had come from her own throat. Something was wrong, very wrong. This was not the way it should be.

Her knees buckled and she crumpled to the floor, as if someone had given her a karate chop from behind. Her fingers clawed at the carpet as she crawled across it to the inert figure a few feet away.

Katherine was on her back, the letter opener protruding obscenely at a right angle from her abdomen, blood oozing from the wound. The front of her lavender nightgown was torn and mottled with the sticky red liquid.

Her eyes were open and stared dully up at Sandra as she bent over her. "Katherine," Sandra sobbed. "Forgive me. Please forgive me!"

Katherine's eyes moved slightly as if in response. "You're alive," Sandra cried, and bent her head to hers. "Thank God, you're still alive!" Sandra's face was wet with tears.

She reached out and tenderly touched Katherine's cheek. "Oh, my darling," she said thickly. "I never meant it to end like this. . . . I did this to you—I did it all. . . . You never killed Stan. I did. . . ."

She felt a tremor go through Katherine's body and looked up at her face. She thought she could read a question in Katherine's eyes and her lips seemed to be trying to form a word, but no sound came out.

"I don't know why I did it," Sandra said, answering the unasked question. "I didn't care about Stan . . . but I wanted to hurt you, make you need me more than ever . . . but you didn't kill him, he was still alive . . . I wanted you to think you had done it . . . and you didn't try to kill me. I did that to myself . . . to make you believe you were crazy . . . but you're not crazy, Katherine. Can you hear me? You're not crazy!"

She searched Katherine's eyes for a sign of acknowledgment. When there was none, her voice became more desperate. "Don't die, my darling," she pleaded. "I won't *let* you die . . . *I'm* the one who should die. I don't deserve to live—I've done terrible things to you . . . but I did them because I loved you. When I couldn't have you, I made you do what I wanted. It was all I could have— but it wasn't enough. So I had to destroy you to make you belong to me. I even went to your father . . . he's so much like you. And I wanted him, too. I could have had him, but he's not *you*, Katherine. No one will ever take your place. Don't die, please don't die, or I'll die, too."

At the mention of her father, Katherine's eyelids had fluttered faintly, but now they were still once again. Her breathing had become increasingly shallow and her face had a masklike pallor. Sandra clutched at her. "Katherine!" When she heard a sigh, she pressed her lips against hers, catching Katherine's breath in her mouth. "I love you, Katherine," she murmured as she took her lips away.

But Katherine had not heard. She was gone. The eyes were now fixed, staring up at Sandra for eternity.

"No!" Sandra cried out. "Don't leave me, Katherine! Please don't leave me!" She put her arms around the body and cradled it to her breast. "You can't leave me," she wailed. "Not now. You're mine forever."

Tears were choking her throat, cutting off the air. Katherine's body was pressing like a weight against her chest and she couldn't breathe. She tried to push Katherine away, but the body flopped back on her. She craned her neck, throwing her head from side to side, her mouth gaping, and the

air came in a rush down her throat. But it was no
use. She had killed Katherine and now it was her
turn. Katherine was being avenged. Blackness
closed in on her, suffocating her, and she knew
she was dying. . . .

MacLaughlin set down his coffee cup, picked
up the phone, and dialed the same number he
had called at least a dozen times this afternoon.
As always, there was no answer.

"Come on, Harry," he said to his partner as he
hung up the phone. "We're going up there."

Harry Gross looked at him. "Do you think we
should get a warrant?"

"Nah, not now," MacLaughlin said. "We can
get one later if we have to."

The two detectives put on their coats and bus-
tled out of the station house. Snow had begun to
fall early in the afternoon, but the rush hour traffic had already turned it a dingy gray. The streets
were slippery, and MacLaughlin forgot about the
two women momentarily as he was forced to concentrate on his driving.

The building was one of those typical East Side
luxury dwellings, with a canopy out front and a
smartly uniformed doorman on duty. The two
men walked into the foyer and showed their
badges to the doorman. "We want to see Katherine
Fielding or Sandra Jurgenson," MacLaughlin said.
He checked his notebook. "Apartment fourteen-F."

"I don't think they're home," the doorman said
meekly.

"Well, try them anyway," MacLaughlin said.

The doorman went to the intercom unit,

pressed the button for 14-F, and picked up the phone. He waited a moment and then pressed the button again. Finally he put down the phone and turned back to the detectives. "They don't answer," he said.

"Have you seen them today?" Gross asked.

"No, I don't think so," the doorman said. "I come on at four o'clock and I usually see them coming home from work about five thirty, six. But I can't remember seeing them this evening."

"Does the super have a key to their apartment?" MacLaughlin asked.

"I—I guess so."

"Then get him out here," MacLaughlin ordered.

The doorman went back to the intercom unit and held a hurried conversation with someone at the other end of the line. "He'll be right out," the doorman said when he was finished.

MacLaughlin and Gross stepped into the lobby, away from the ears of the doorman.

"Looks like they skipped out," Gross said.

"Yeah," MacLaughlin agreed. "I called their office twice this afternoon. Seems Jurgenson never came back from lunch. But it sure doesn't look like they're here. I'd say we've got ourselves two prime suspects."

"Think they're both in it, or is one just protecting the other?"

"Hard to say. But when I saw that blonde this morning she was real nervous—and she sure didn't want me to talk to her roommate."

Just then a short, gray-haired man in a baggy sweater approached them. "Are you the police?" he asked.

The men nodded and showed him their badges. "We want to get into apartment 14-F," MacLaughlin said.

"Well, I, uh—do you have a warrant?" the man asked timidly.

"No, but we can get one if we need to," MacLaughlin said, putting on his best "long arm of the law" manner.

"Well, I don't know," the man said, scratching his head. "You really should have a warrant."

"Look, we'll get one if it'll make you happy," Gross said, "but all you're doing is causing us unnecessary delay. This is a homicide case and those two women are important to the investigation."

"Homicide, huh?" the man said, obviously impressed. "Well, in that case, I guess I'd better let you in. Only I think they have another lock on their door and I don't have a key to that one."

"Let's just go up and see," MacLaughlin said, leading the way across the lobby.

At the door to 14-F the super pointed to a metal plate surrounding a second lock. "You see," he said, "that's a dead-bolt lock and I don't have a key for it, so I can't let you in."

"Okay," MacLaughlin said impatiently. "If we have to, we'll get a locksmith *and* a warrant, but maybe they didn't lock the second lock, so let's just try it."

The super hesitated. "Don't you think we better ring first? Maybe they're home and they just didn't hear the doorman buzzing them."

MacLaughlin jabbed at the doorbell several times with his finger. "Satisfied?" he said to the super when no one answered it. "Okay, try it," he said, pointing to the primary lock.

The super fitted his key in and turned it. The door opened easily.

"Well, whadya know?" Gross said. "They must have left in some hurry if they didn't bother to double-lock the door."

The super stepped into the apartment. "Miss Fielding? Miss Jurgenson?" he called out. "It's Ralph, the super. There are two policemen with me." He was greeted by absolute silence.

MacLaughlin and Gross stepped into the apartment behind him. Gross peered into the kitchen on their right. "Nothin'," he said, turning back to MacLaughlin.

The super was standing near the dining room table, fidgeting with his keys. "You know they're both such nice girls," he said. "I sure hope they're not in trouble."

The detectives ignored him as they surveyed the empty, quiet living room. "You check in there," MacLaughlin said to Gross, indicating a door off to the left. "I'll take the one over here." He walked to a doorway on the right.

MacLaughlin walked through the doorway and froze in his tracks. In all his years on the force he had never seen a sight quite like this one. It was not the naked dead girl on the floor who shocked him, but the living one, kneeling by her side.

Her face and arms were completely smeared with dried blood and her blond hair was caked with it. The front of her lavender nightgown was bloodstained and there was a long tear in it, from the middle down to the hem. She was holding the hand of the corpse, talking softly to it, and seemed to be unaware that there was anybody else in the room.

The nude woman had apparently been dead for some time. A shiny blade protruded from her abdomen. As MacLaughlin stepped closer, he could make out the letter "H" on the ornate handle of the blade.

"Harry," MacLaughlin called out. "Get in here."

Gross appeared at the door, followed by the super.

"Oh, my God!" the super burst out. He clapped his hand over his mouth and quickly turned away.

"There's our letter opener," MacLaughlin said, pointing to the body. "I can't tell if she did it herself or if the other one did it."

Gross stared at the kneeling figure. "What the hell did she do to herself?" he muttered. "Jesus, it looks like she washed herself in blood."

"Yeah, and she's in shock, that's for sure," MacLaughlin said. "You'd better call this one in, and I'll try to get her out of here."

Gross left and MacLaughlin stepped around the body. Bending down, he looked at the girl's face. If this was Katherine Fielding, she must have been very beautiful when she was alive.

He looked at the other girl, puzzled. He thought she was Sandra Jurgenson, but he could not be sure. She looked so different from the way he had seen her this morning—even apart from the blood that obscured her features. Her blond hair had been shoulder-length then, and now it was cut short. But it was more than just her hair. She almost looked like a different person.

MacLaughlin took her arm and gently pulled her to her feet. She was still clinging to the dead girl's hand, and MacLaughlin had to pry her fingers free. He found a bathrobe and put it around her shoulders. Then he led her, step by step, out of the bedroom and into the living room, where he sat her down on the couch. Her eyes did not acknowledge his presence; they remained as vacant as before.

He doubted that he would get any answers out of her now, in her state of extreme shock. But just for the record, he had to try. He sat down beside her. "Can you talk?" he asked.

He was surprised when she answered clearly, "Yes, of course, I can."

He took out his notebook. "Then can you tell me what happened?"

"Nothing happened." Her voice was calm, even.

"Then what's that in the bedroom?" he prodded.

"I don't know what you're talking about," she answered blankly.

"Now, Mrs. Jurgenson—"

"Why do you call me that?" she asked.

MacLaughlin shook his head. The girl was obviously too confused to talk. Didn't even know her own name. He shut his notebook, got up and went over to his partner. The two men stood there, talking in low voices and looking at her.

She stared at them, and then her eyes went to the portrait on the opposite wall. *Fools.* Couldn't they see the resemblance? She drew her knee up